Dante's London Bridge

A novella by Peter Prizel
Word count: 21544

Introduction

Dante's London Bridge is a novella set in England during the reign of Henry VIII. It is a re-imagining of the famous narrative poem written by Durante di Alighiero degli Alighieri, The Divine Comedy. While Dante chose to pen his work in colloquial language in 1321, Dante's London Bridge is written using the "vernacular" of 2025. It is told with humor, through the use of email, telegrams, poetry (written by the forsaken Virgil himself), free verse poetry (with pop culture references), and a "Head's Chorus" complete with musical charts. Dante's discourse on human nature and society's biassed and discriminatory hierarchy is as relevant, if not more so, today as it was 700 years ago.

List of characters and their locations in Hell, Purgatory or Paradise
(in order of appearance)

Character:	Place of Residence:
Virgil	Hell: Limbo
Ciacco	Hell: Circle of Gluttony
Arnus	Hell: Circle of Fraud
Belaccqua	Ante-Purgatory
King David	Terrace of Pride Purgatory
Madam Francesca	Hell: Circle of Lust
Muhammad	Hell: Circle of Schismatics
Bruno Latini	Hell: Circle of Sodomites
Charon	Oarsman of River Thames
Sapia	Terrace of Envy: Purgatory
Forese Doanti	Terrace of Gluttony Purgatory
Anonymous Soul	Hell: Circle of Greed
Fillipo Argenti	Hell: Circle of Wrath
Lord Uberti	Hell: Circle of the Heretics
Guido Guinizzelli	Terrace of Lust: Purgatory
Pope Adrian V	Terrace of Greed: Purgatory
Alexander the Great	Hell: Circle of Violence
Hugh Capet	Terrace of Avarice: Purgatory
Piccarda Donati	Paradise: Sphere of the Moon
King Manfred	Terrace of the Excommunicate: Purgatory
Iacopo del Cassero	Terrace of the Late-Repentant: Purgatory
Constantine	Paradise: Sphere of Jupiter
St. Benedict	Paradise: Sphere of Saturn
Dante Allegri	Paradise: God themself
Cacciacuida	Paradise: Sphere of Mars
St. Thomas	Paradise: Sphere of the Sun
St. Peter	Paradise: Sphere of the Stars
Charels Martel	Paradise: Sphere of Venus
The Angels	Paradise: The Primum Mobile
Justinian	Paradise: Sphere of Mercury

PROLOGUE OR THE BRIDGE CONUNDRUM

From the windows of the Chapel of St Thomas Becket
the moon caresses the fog. Soughing branches creak
over London Bridge. The Thames roars under.
I hear the cries below. I see boils on the backs
of souls oozing pus into an unforgiving river.
The sins run downstream like the corpses of
salmon who have just mated. In the chapel
I count clinking coins
Effigies of sovereignty
return my stare. I'm the
warden of this bridge.
Here, languishing souls
are purified under god's
gaze and justice's ears.
Now a funeral barge. The bodies
of headless men bedecked in sackcloth,
they seek passage to under my causeway's jaws–
the drawbridge to paradise. Their heads hang upon
the viaduct. They plead their case while my tenants decry
their enterprise.
What's a warden to do?

Head's Chorus

for Piano Trio

We did noth-ing wrong but we fell vict - um to Hen - ry's whims

un - ab - le to give him a male heir. the church he did not spare

Thus, we hang on pikes for all to see, a war - ning woe to thee

From the desk of Virgil – Poet and Warden of Old London Bridge

The souls of Hell condemned to eternity in the River Thames are exchanging letters. The impetus for this flurry of activity is most strange. I had just finished counting the collections from the day's tolls. I was just settling down to bed in St Thomas Becket's Chapel, where I have
been afforded a small cot and was about to write in my diary, when I caught sight of a barge with headless bodies on it near the bridge, seeking passage, The only comfort I have, aside from supposedly being in the bosom of God (a god whom I do not know as I am a pagan), is that my apartment is always warm since it sits over the burning sarcophagus of one of the souls condemned to Hell Although it floats in the Thames, the heat is so great that, even in the dead of winter, I feel warm.

In my living hours I was a poet, a good one, an undiscovered artist, yet into eternity I bring the terrible memories of my failures, total obscurity. But what do I now have to lose? Perhaps it is time I pick up my pen again. Perhaps in my afterlife, success will find me.

How I got assigned to be the warden of the bridge is beyond me.

I cannot help but feel a mixture of contempt and superiority to those Hellish Souls in the river around that barge of bodies. Let's forget that they are damned for eternity. But then again so I am, which plays into my resentment. You see I did not have the opportunity to accept Christ as I lived before he was even born. I am in a limbo that I cannot get out of. The only difference is that I do not suffer. Still, I am denied access to heaven. My resentment is augmented by the fact that the Hellish Souls seem to think that their form of communication, their letters, are works of art. Actually, they are atrocious. I once tried to read them my poetry, and they said it was laughable. Why can't anyone see the virtue in my poetry?

What are letters but a bunch of emotions vomited on paper? There is nothing creative. Their letters are nothing more than an unstructured stream of thoughts. There are no hidden meanings in their texts, no double entendres.

If I were among the condemned I wouldn't want to do comparative bitching with other souls. What else could the souls in the river be writing about? Yes, there is a pair that is married down there, condemned to the Circle of Lust, but even their letters are nothing more than sweet nothings. What a waste of paper!

The bodies are those of people who in King Henry VIII's twisted mind committed high treason, as they did not back his divorcing Catherine of Aragon. King Henry had the poor creatures thrown in the Tower of London before beheading them. The bodies' heads are impaled upon Old London Bridge, warning others not to defy the king. Often the heads talk, and now their chatter seems to be incessant as they are excited about seeing their bodies. The excitement is so palpable.

But back to the letters. I sense that you are going to be bored with them, so let me try to induce you to do so with an open mind by telling you a little about their authors. The first writer in this "chain" of dialogue in letters is none other than Arnus, a soul condemned to The Circle Of Fraud – but more about him later.

The letter which Arnus has written is addressed to Signore Ciacco. Ciacco is a coin clinker. The sounds of coins rubbing together, that was the music that made him rise with the sun and dream when the moon came up. His mind was gluttonous, a repository for greed. When the Florentine banker was alive, he was known as "The Pig." Supposedly, he was as fat as King Henry VIII himself.

Ciacco, the poor soul, did not repent before death, and therefore could not divorce his sins as Henry had recently divorced his wife. Now Ciacco is condemned to Dante's third circle of Hell - Gluttony. Here Ciacco dwells in shit, next to Cerberus whose barks ensure that he cannot get a wink of sleep even if he were able to handle the smell.

Ah, I am inspired to write:

Fetid gases caress Ciacco's nostrils
the deafening barks of Cerberus ring
in his ears.

A nauseating frothy contemptuous brew
over a hovel of muck. The rinds of sin, they are
the souls shit in which they must live.

On Earth, Ciacco was a banker dressed in silks.
Every evening he stared at the dead pig
on the inlaid olivewood table, licking his lips.

The banker consumed the swine.
He ate so much that his waist matches Henry's girth.
But, unlike the King, it is too late to divorce sin.

I thank you for indulging me my creative endeavors. Now, are you wondering how I am able to read the contents of the letters?

I work with Charon, the Greek God who ferries souls on his skiff below the bridge for a fee. How the souls led their lives when they were one with their bodies determines where Charon drops them off. If they are destined for Hell, Charon drops them at their assigned spot in the Thames; if for Purgatory, he drops them off at the door under my chapel near the waterline. When there is a knock, I meet the soul and lead it to its appropriate station on Old London Bridge.

Finally, if the soul has led a virtuous life, Charon ferries it across the river to Parliament, where the soul assumes its seat as an advisor to the Prime Minister, God. Charon is also the postman for the souls of Hell. I was given the privilege of reading the letter before it reached its intended recipient. Allow me to share it with you.

February 2nd
Anno Domini 1533
(The Year of our Lord. ???
unnecessary)

From:
Mr. Arnus (Diviner of the Stars)
PO Box: Eighth Circle of Hell
Apt: Fraud
666

To:
Mr. Ciacco (Gluttonous Banker of Florence)
PO Box: Third Circle of Hell
Apt: Gluttony
666

My Dear Ciacco,

As I am sure you have heard the divorce proceedings of King Henry and Catherine of Aragon have been completed. It was so messy, so treacherous. To be honest, it would not surprise me at all if when the King meets his maker he is assigned far below us in the circle of treachery. Be that as it may, Catherine is not his only victim. Did you see the barge of headless souls this evening? I've no doubt they are the Cardinal and Chancellor and other officials who opposed the dissolution of the royal marriage. I hear Henry has put on many pounds since his divorce - his waist is now some fifty- inches. He can almost compete with you. Do you think that you would like his company when he meets his demise, or would you prefer that he go to the circle of treachery mentioned above.

Very Truly Yours,

Arnus

From the desk of Virgil – Poet and Warden of Old London Bridge
HELL- The Circle of Fraud (Fourth Bolgia or ditch)

I imagine that the letter you just read piqued your interest, and, if it didn't, you should know that it did mine.

Once again, I am driven to create:

ARNUS

In death you see what you could not in life.
Your once shunned anus' sphincter–
the bubble of your oculus. The mire
of dung unintelligible and blinding.

On Earth you once read stars time upon
time and times again. Gold paid to you
weighed your hand to the ground
under which you lie forever.

Now you walk backwards, aping
the past when you have no future.

I know what you are probably thinking. Who would write a poem about someone who has their head up their ass? I'll bet you think that such a venture is as shallow as the letters that are being written by the Hellish souls. I thought I would try as I never have shown anyone my poetry from beyond the grave. Anyway, here is my biography, if you will, of Arnus in plain old prose so you can see who we are dealing with.

Good old Arnus, he was so smart in life. He would tell farmers he knew when they should plant their crops by reading the stars. Arnus was a diviner and would charge fees for his "services." In his mortal life, Arnus looked only outwards and used the sky to deceive others so that, in death, God has made him look inwards. Now he wanders, walking backwards with his head up his ass. I think that it is only appropriate that Arnus started the letters. Perhaps he can relate to the headless bodies better than any other Hellish soul in the Thames as he is essentially headless himself. I am going to have to go to confession more often with all the mail I am intercepting and opening, but I sense it may be for a good cause. May God forgive me, for opening the mail. I thank him for letting me live in the Chapel of St Thomas Becket where I have an altar to ask for forgiveness.

February 7th
Anno Domini 1533

From:
Mr. Ciacco (Gluttonous Banker of Florence)
PO Box: Third Circle of Hell
Apt: Gluttony
666

To:
Mr. Arnus (Diviner of the Stars)
PO Box: Eighth Circle of Hell
Apt: Fraud
666

Dear Arnus,

You are truly living up to your condemnation of wandering around till the end of time with your head up your ass! It should be obvious to you that these headless bodies seeking passage under London Bridge are martyrs on their way to Paradise. It is imperative that we help them secure safe passage under the bridge. This will have to be a collaborative effort. I will continue writing letters to the other seven souls that reside with us in the Thames. I propose that you assist me. I will write to Francesca and Fillipo, and those in the circle of Avarice who have been deemed unrecognizable, those who have been punished by God as having no physical identity due to their greed for money. You take care of the rest.

Your Humble Servant

Ciacco

PS: I will also write to Virgil, the warden of the bridge. As you know, we need his (and that of the souls on Old London Bridge) help to raise it.

**From the desk of Virgil – Poet and Warden of Old London Bridge
The layout of Old London Bridge and a description of Ante-
Purgatory, the lowest level of Mt Purgatory, where souls who have
led negligent lives reside. The story of Belacqua.**

I am finally being acknowledged. Ciacco knows that my help will be needed. As you know, I live on Old London Bridge and I am its warden. We charge tolls for both crossing in the water and on land. The shops on the bridge are crammed together, and one can hear through the walls. They hang precariously over the sides of the bridge clinging like icicles to eaves in the winter. They are made of stone as we learned from the fires of the past. They range from everything from needle- makers to haberdashers.

The shops are set atop a straight line of nineteen arches with a drawbridge in the middle, this hub of commerce. This is London's Purgatory. Here the shop keepers do penance until they can go to Parliament, which as I mentioned before, is a place where one can speak their mind freely without having to worry if they have offended morality or God. This Paradise lies across the river.

The shops are set atop a straight line of nineteen arches with a drawbridge in the middle, this hub of commerce. This is London's Purgatory. Here the shop keepers do penance until they can go to Parliament, which as I mentioned before, is a place where one can speak their mind freely without having to worry if they have offended morality or God. This Paradise lies across the river.

The telegrams often are not even written in full sentences. They are bone-dry, the writing is surgical and speaks only of wants and needs. There is no tension, no nuance. The writing is juvenile, even more so than in the letters. If my heart were not so good I wouldn't bother to deliver them, but I do. And alright, yes, I do have a modicum of hope that if I do so God may look kindly upon me and get me out of this limbo. Just as there are nine Hellish Souls in the river, there are nine souls on this bridge, one from every terrace of Purgatory.

One who is in Ante-Purgatory for being lazy is Belacqua. In life, he was a musician, friend to Dante, himself. He was lazy and lived off the backs of others; now he is a bookseller. Thank God he repented before his death. His life was as nondescript as this short poem I have composed about him.

he broke his harp strings
kept the tortoiseshell – forgot
the hard guts of life

ST THOMAS BECKET CHAPEL
OLD LONDON BRIDGE

FROM: BELACQUA, HEAD OF BOOKSELLERS GUILD ON LONDON BRIDGE

TO: HIS MAJESTY KING DAVID, KEEPER OF THE HEADS

YOUR MAJESTY, I KNOW I AM THE LAZY ONE - STOP - BUT PUT DOWN YOUR HARP AND HEAR ME OUT AS WE ARE FELLOW MUSICIANS - STOP - THE SOULS OF HELL ARE PLOTTING TO LET THIS BARGE THROUGH - STOP - I ALREADY SEE CHARON THE FERRY MAN THAT TAKES THE DEAD TO THEIR AFTERLIFE FERRYING LETTERS BETWEEN THEM AS THEY DISCUSS THEIR NEFARIOUS PLOT – STOP -

RESPECTFULLY,

BELACQUA (THE HARP MAKER WHO WASTED HIS LIFE)

Heads' Chorus

for Piano

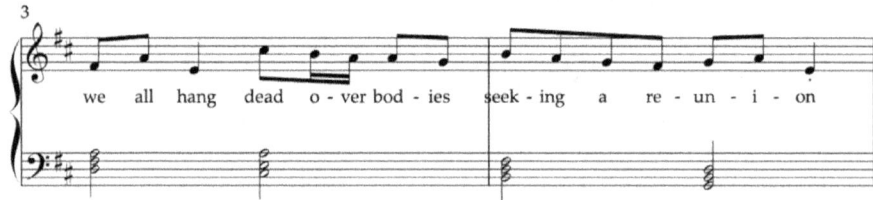

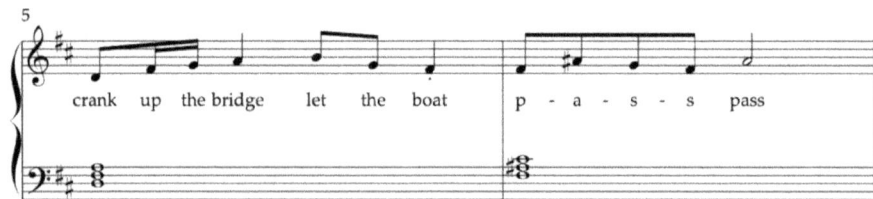

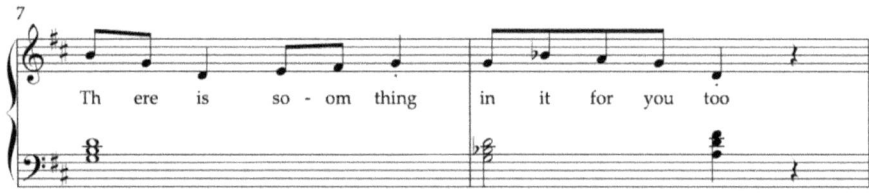

From the Desk of Virgil - Poet and Warden of Old London Bridge
PURGATORY – TERRACE OF PRIDE – KING DAVID

I am supposed to believe a bunch of preserved heads when they say that there is something in it for me?

Up on the pikes there are four of them. There's Anne Bolyen, Henry's second wife, executed for failing to produce a male heir. Then there is his fifth wife, Katherine Howard, whose life was cut short after Henry discovered that she had committed adultery. There is Thomas Moore who refused to recognize Henry as the head of the church. Finally, there is Thomas Cromwell, executed for treason. So there, you have been introduced to the cast of singers whose aria you just heard. But back to the telegrams.

You must have been surprised when you saw that Belacqua's telegram was to none other than King David, himself. Believe me, I was surprised when I found out he was in Purgatory, and Dante was even more so. Why is he there? He is so out of place. If anything, he should be in Hell with the murderers for indirectly killing Uriah so he could marry the soldier's wife. Or he should be in Paradise for founding the house from which the Messiah sprung. But no, David and his trusty harp are in Purgatory.

Well, the answer is that David danced amongst his people in front of the arc even after he had Uriah killed. A murderer has no place doing this, but David, thinking his kinship gave him a carte-blanche, did so anyway. David has been the keeper of the heads long before I was the warden. Given his transgression of murder, it is only fitting. Every night I watch him dance the maypole with them. I've been invited to participate but I always decline. To me the dance is nothing more than a Danse Macabre, since he is a murderer, and those heads are of murdered souls.

I once asked David how he does his job as it is so morbid. He told me that to him it is not as if he feels he is helping others from falling under another king's murderous acts of executions. To me such an answer is a cop out, but to each his own. Oh, before I divulge the contents of the telegram let me show you the poem I wrote about King Daivd. It is so beautiful and so concise. How I can say everything in three short stanzas but try I shall.

PURGATORY –TERRACE OF PRIDE KING DAVID

Jessie's son David did not thank God.
So, he dances macabre before
a golden ark.

Shackled to the laws
he should have followed,
which his crown and orb hijacked.

See how his feet move–fast
as if over coals. The heavy-
handed law unmerciful

Jessie's son, David did not thank God.
So, he dances macabre before
a golden ark.

ST THOMAS BECKET CHAPEL
OLD LONDON BRIDGE

FROM: KING DAVID KEEPER OF THE HEADS

TO: BELACQUA HEAD OF THE MUSICAL INSTRUMENT
GUILD

BELACQUA - STOP - I AM IN RECEIPT OF YOUR
TELEGRAM - STOP - THE HEADS ARE PITCHING QUITE
A FIT - STOP - WE NEED TO SPEAK WITH VIRGIL - STOP
- DON'T DO ANYTHING UNTIL HE DELIVERS THE
OTHER TELEGRAMS - STOP

HIS MAJESTY

DAVID (PRIDEFUL SOUL)

From the desk of Virgil – Poet and Warden of Old London Bridge
HELL – THE CIRCLE OF LUST

If that telegram which I just delivered is nothing more than a piece of self-centered writing, I don't know what is. But on to lust.

I am sure you all have heard of it, if not experienced it in some shape or form. Lust is the first circle of Hell. The feeling is such an engrained, biologically driven part of our instinctual selves; I think that is why Dante made it the least grave of all sins. Still, there is that Francesca da Rimini, immortalized in The Comedy, who fell in love with her husband's already-married younger brother, Paola. The marriage to her husband was purely political, no emotions or attractions were involved on her part. The taking up with her brother-in-law as an outlet for her needs condemned her to Dante's first circle of Hell. Here she spins around forever chasing her lover, carried away by a harsh wind, whose velocity matches the fevered lust that dictated her life when she carried on with Paolo on Earth.

When I look down at Francesca and Paolo, I feel they have been given some reprieve. Still, only inches above the surface of the river, they barely avoid grazing the pus-filled wounds of great sinners and the mire in which they float. Yes, their flight pattern, dictated by harsh winds in perennial circles, is monotonous but it sure beats being in the river itself. Still, I pity them. Francesca no doubt would have been loyal to whomever she'd married had she had that choice. Perhaps that is why she is in a limbo of sorts just above the river. Not bad enough to be directly in Hell, but not good enough to avoid being subject to its facade.

Old Ciacco thinks he can put Francesca to use in wooing Charon. That is why he has written to her. If anyone can get the ferryman of the dead, that stiff, to do anything it would be her.

Those souls in Hell, they have no shame. I doubt they even care that I read their letters as they have nothing to lose. They will never advance beyond their damnation. I don't fully understand their motives. Then, again, I don't fully understand the behavior of those souls in Purgatory here on Old London Bridge. They say that souls can shave off time in Purgatory if prayers are offered for them. Why don't they ever come to my church and pray for each other? No one comes here to confess either. I wonder if the souls on the bridge would do it if they knew it would shorten their sentence. It would make sense.

Sometimes I wonder if I would make a good priest. When I am down and want to be alone, I often sit inside the confession booth and contemplate my life after death, the life that I am living now. As a poet I wrote about life. I think I would be pretty good at wading through the penitent's woes. The only question is what God or gods would work through me. I hear that priests are God's instruments and that they act as his representative when preaching or performing sacraments. I hear they have but one God, a one-size-fits-all concept. Supposedly this God, whoever he is, lives in Parliament or Paradise. If you stand on the bridge, you can see the Parliament Building from any angle. It is always lit up like some beacon on a hill shining down on the sinners in the river and the souls on Old London Bridge in Purgatory. I hear that this God is forgiving and that his name is Dante. The name sounds Italian. Maybe Dante hails from the same region of Italy as I do. Still, I am a creature of habit, so I have not yet submitted to this God, to this Dante. Can he really offer me anything of worth?

If I were to sit in this booth as a priest, I would not know on whom to call upon. Would it be Zeus, the king of the gods? Or perhaps Apollo, the God of Truth, as the penitent are confessing their deepest, ugliest truths. Maybe it would be Ares the God of war, as the penitent are declaring war on sin. Who knows? I might try my hand at being one who grants absolution one day. But back to the letters. Here is my poem about poor Francesca and her lover.

When the meteors cross in the darkness
they hide their faces.
A millisecond of vision is too much to bear.
They leave their blind tails to languish
over the Themes to listen to the moans.

The tornado of Francesca chasing Paolo.
An eternal tornado of misguided feelings,
viral proteins unable to latch onto a cell.

The waters of the Themes lap
her triangular loins. The sinful
waters trying to give what Paolo
did in life.

She'll never catch him. Her hound
of desire will never bring back the kill.

I think the third stanza still needs some cleaning up. But I do like the couplet at the end. What do you think?

February 9th
Anno Domini 1533

From:
Mr. Ciacco (Gluttonous Banker of Florence)
PO Box: Third Circle of Hell
Apt: Gluttony
666

To:
Madam Francesca (Adulterous Maiden)
PO Box: First Circle of Hell
Apt: Lust
666

Francesca,

I know you have never been one for necrophilia, either now or when you were alive. You've been swirling around in a wind chasing after Paolo's ghost ever since you died. Or is he chasing after you? Anyway, it does not matter. We need you to jump Charon's bones. I sense the souls up on Old London Bridge, the ones in Purgatory, are going to give us hell (no pun intended) about getting these martyred bodies under the bridge. Our only option may be to use skiffs. So, turn on the charm.

Ciao,

Ciaccio

February 10th
Anno Domini 1533

From:
Madam Francesca (Adulterous Maiden)
PO Box: First Circle of Hell
Apt: Lust
666

To:
Mr. Ciacco (Gluttonous Banker of Florence)
PO Box: Third Circle of Hell
Apt: Gluttony
666

Ciaccio,

I looked at Charon yesterday when I got your letter. Although Charon is as haggard and ugly as he always has been, he is nowhere near as repulsive as you. I'd rather ride a headless body than him. Of course, I could do reverse cowgirl with him, but the smell of death would make me faint. Why don't you write to Bruno Latini and see if he is game for this cock-eyed ???venture??? of yours.

Francesca

PS: I do empathize with the headless bodies, though, and hear Thomas Moore was quite a looker.

From the desk of Virgil – Poet and Warden of Old London Bridge
HELL – THE CIRCLE OF FRAUD (8th Bolgia or ditch)

It seems that Ciacco's overtures to Francesca have failed. I had expected her to slap him in the face, but I guess she restrained herself. Were she here on the bridge in Purgatory, I am sure that God would have considered her lack of action to be a sign of penance which could have gotten her closer to Paradise. But alas, she is in Hell, so that does not seem to be an option.

So Ciacco is sent back to the drawing board. He is such a typical male to have chosen lust as his first attempt to solve the problem at hand. I must say that I am amazed that Arnus, that pitiful soul who has his head up his ass, seems to be more intelligent than that pig from Florence!

In his letter, not only does Arnus ask Muhammad for help, but he also dates his letter in the way the Muslims do. He must be trying to flatter him. Muhammad is in the circle of schismatics who are fraudulent in their faith according to Dante. Islam, that religion out of Arabia. I am not sure what to think of it. But we do need to create a schism in Charon's mind between what he thinks his only job is and the more important job we need him to do. For, as I said, he only ferries the dead sent to Hell, and he must be convinced to ferry the dead bodies on the barge to Paradise in Parliament. So, as I said, I have to hand it to Arnus for asking Muhammad for help. For what does this "prophet" have to lose by such a proposition? He might even gain by converting Charon to Islam.

Poor Muhammad - all he did was listen to Jabril (Gabriel) in a cave and tell the masses what he had heard. Now he wanders in circles around his Bolgia only to be hacked in half when he reaches his starting point. I can see why Dante meted out this punishment since Islam had

been a burning wound in the side of Christianity for centuries. I
hope this changes in the future. Whenever he approaches the
blade, held by a demon, Muhammad's eyes turn inward as if
crossed. Through gritted teeth and a furrowed brow, he repeats the
Surahs of the Quran as if expecting some divine intervention to
save him, only to feel the cold steal again. The poor man cannot
even die a martyr's death. I doubt that any of his followers have
even read the Divine Comedy. Still the prophet's faith never falters.
But it must never have crosser his that a prophet would have
wound up in hell and not at the side of his creator. I've read many
poems about Christ and his stigmata, but writing about
Muhammad's pain and suffering is challenging. It's in its very
preliminary stages so don't be too judgmental.

THE WOUNDED ARABIAN

Dante followed the rules of Islam. He did not
depict Muhammad's full image. The torso of
The Seal of The Prophets perpetually cut by
Demons, thus He is never seen as a whole
in the circle to which he is condemned.

What is a religion if not a fermented cult?
How strong is the proof that the adherent has to drink?
How many Arabian grains of sand must get in the eyes
until one sees the way?

Under the knife, the Prophet screams neither the cries
of war or of peace.
He weeps in agony over his the enthralls. For over them
which he cannot
practice haruspicy.

February 11th
Hijri Era 940

From:
Mr. Arnus (Diviner of the Stars)
PO Box: Eighth Circle of Hell
Apt: Fraud
666

To:
Mr. Muhammad (Schismatic of the Church)
PO Box: Eighth Circle of Hell
Apt: Schismatics
666

Muhammad,

Peace Be Upon You. I hope you respond to this letter. As you know it was certified mail. Your assistance is needed in helping convince Charon to ferry these headless souls to Paradise. He has never had headless customers. I think that he does not believe that they are worthy of Heaven. The bodies, they may not be Muslims, but they are People of the Book. I know you will help. Isn't it odd how now we are in Hell we all feel contrite. If only we had felt that during our time on Earth.

Inshallah,

Arnus

February 11th
Hijri Era 940

From:
Mr. Muhammad (Schismatic of the Church)
PO Box: Eighth Circle of Hell
Apt: Schismatics
666

To:
Mr. Arnus
PO Box: Eighth Circle of Hell
Apt: Fraud
666

Arnus,

Al salama alaykum. I could have just walked over and knocked on your door. You may be on a different terrace than me in Fraud, but we have the same landlord. Did Dante raise your rent? If he did, I will ensure that you stop paying me jizya for subletting the ground floor to my apartment. My empathies certainly do lie with those headless bodies on the barge and their severed heads on the bridge. They deserve to see Paradise, and so do you. If only you were not anatomically challenged, if only you could see clearly and did not have your head up your ass. Which makes me wonder how you were able to write this letter? In any case. I'll speak with Charon and keep you posted. I hope this note finds you well.

Praise Allah,

Muhammad

From the desk of Virgil – Poet and Warden of Old London Bridge

Ah, I am so tired that I have to vent as this postmaster business is exhausting. What do you think of this poem? It's called Messages.

MESSAGES

In life as a poet I strove to pare down lines–
But not here. In death,
The laws of verse are suspended
on Old London Bridge.

The pig's fat consumes the wick
of the candle I left lit when I went out.
Out to deliver letters, to deliver telegrams
Words of nothingness. Letters trapped
in folded ravines of parchment. Means
written to ends that I cannot understand.

I've been walking all day
I come home under a sickle moon
cutting into my tired muscles.
They have traversed Purgatory,
traversed Old London Bridge
this hellish Hellespont
in mid London dozens of times.

The candle is out. A new batch
Of mail is on my bed. But I have no rest.
I read the letters. My eyes singed with
anger at the gibberish written on the parchment,
They enlist my tongue–
But not to write poetry.

They employ it as a servant.
A servant to lick and reseal the envelopes
that I will deliver when the sun rises.

From the desk of Virgil – Poet and Warden of Old London Bridge
HELL – THE SODOMITES (SEVENTH CIRCLE)

It seems that Ciacco does not learn. In this next letter he may be asking "the other side, those who love the same sex" to help him with Charon, but the request is again entirely based on Lust. I don't know whether to laugh or cry. I also must say that I spoke prematurely when I praised Francesca. I forgot that it was she who advised the Florentine Banker to write to Brunetto Latini in the first place.

I am tired of Ciacco's antics. So, after saying my prayers I retreat to my bed in the chapel. I'll deliver his letter tomorrow. All the torches in London are out. All the debates in that beacon on the hill - in Parliament, the house of Paradise, the house of God, that they call Dante - are done for the day. Still, in spite of my profound fatigue, I have trouble sleeping. Under arch thirteen which is parallel to my chapel under arch twelve, the river slows ever so slightly, thanks to two half-rotten skiffs that did not make it through at high tide. These rotten boats make the water slow. The sodomites decamped here as it is just out of view of Parliament and The Tower of London.

Ashamed to be seen, their punishment, the hell fire which singes their backs, still follows then raining down pain. The fire, its acrid smoke tickles my nose and burns my chest, and its light keeps me awake. The balls of fire fly behind the stained-glass window of The Blessed Mother right above my bed, making her veil look like a demonic head piece. The fire has decapitated her comforting gaze. Across from her, on the opposite wall facing the foot of my bed, is Christ. In winter, the icicles grow behind the stained-glass window of Jesus, making it appear as if he has frozen locks of hair.

If only Bruno would go back under arch nineteen. He is not saving face; everyone knows what he did. He went against the sacred act of reproduction, but at least this rendered him childless, so he does not have a legacy. Perhaps in later days, views of his cohorts and him will change. Maybe the bridge of altruistic love will grow wider and more accepting. But ever since it was rebuilt in stone, Old London Bridge is set in its ways, standing above the Hellish Thames in judgment while housing the penitent above. I rise from my bed and make my way to my small desk. I push aside the parchments with the year's accounting of the tolls. I light a candle and reopen the envelope and read the letter again. I am so disgusted I cannot decide whether I want to burn it or save it with the other letters (I have been copying them for myself into my diary) or publish it along with the other letters. I bet if I were to combine all these letters and telegrams into a book that it would be a best seller. It seems that the more sensationalist something is, the more likely it is to sell. But before I do, I'll let you read it and decide if it should be consigned to the flames. Oh – I almost forgot the poem. Is this one worthy of saving? Or should I burn it as well?

THE SODMITES

The rudder steers the ship wrong.
The prow dashes on the rocks,
Making the whaler's wife mourn
on her widow's balcony.
Through the storm of Hell's fire
goes the captain who could
not keep his feelings in the brig.

Brunetto, ambassador of love who could
not keep his distance now pays the captain's
price–In a foreign land.

Poetry is sometimes about "The art of the unsaid". One does not want to always come down like a sledgehammer to the reader. How do you think I did in this regard?

February 13th
Anno Domini 1533

From:
Mr. Ciacco (Gluttonous Banker of Florence)
PO Box: Third Circle of Hell
Apt: Gluttony
666

To:
Brunetto Latini (Sodomite)
PO Box: Seventh Circle of Hell
C/O Third Ring of the Circle
Apt: Homosexuality
666

Greetings Bruno! I hope you are well. Francesca advised that I write to you, and ask for a favor she cannot, or is unwilling to provide. I am sure you are aware of the tenuous position of the souls of the funeral barge near Old London Bridge. We need Charon's assistance. Francesca could have beat a dead horse and had the favor returned on behalf of the poor headless bodies on the barge, but she refuses. Could you possibly rise to the occasion?

Cheers,

Ciaccio

February 14th
Anno Domini 1533

From:
Brunetto Latini (Sodomite)
PO Box: Seventh Circle of Hell
C/O Third Ring of the Circle
Apt: Homosexuality
666

To:
Madam Francesca (Adulterous Maiden)
PO Box: First Circle of Hell
Apt: Lust
666

Francesca,

I know you won't find me writing to you a surprise as I do so every Valentines Day. I also write to all the other souls in this hellish freezing river. This is also nothing new to you. However, I must tell you that this year I chose to write to you first. Now, before you feel all flattered and write back to thank me, read below.

I have a bone to pick with you. Apparently, you advised that swine, Ciaccio, to write me to see if I would do what you would not. I can understand that you do not find Charon worthy of a lay, nor do I. But to assume that I would find him attractive, and to kick the can down the road to me - that is unforgivable. If you were not dead, I would say that you belong in the lowest branch of the circles of Hell, Treachery Against Friends. However, I am willing to overlook your transgression in the interest of helping the headless bodies.

I hope Cupid hits you when you look at Charon next, then we do not need to carry this discussion any further.

Bruno

PS: We have to be very careful about how we interact with Charon. Should word get around that our proclivities are the reason he listens to us it will be most embarrassing.

From the desk of Virgil – Poet and Warden of Old London Bridge

CHARON

The skiff slides sullenly over the Themes.
Baggy flesh covers the cage that shrouds
his heart, as the envelopes do the letters.
The helmsman he's out of his element,
and so are the souls he watches. What
would Dante do if his body was on
the skiff head and all? Would he have a solution?

Who knows. God's body lies in Ravenna.
 An endless stream of olive oil from Florence flows
by his tomb – the city's tears.
The products of cries uttered for having exiled
its finest sun that Ravenna refuses to let set.
If the oarsman changes course, if
his heart waxes, if the selfishness
of my tenants wane, I'll open the
drawbridge.

What did you think of that little piece of verse? It's okay if you aren't blown away by it. I have done several drafts and sense that I will have to do many more. I sense that you now have a feeling about the strong misgivings I have about opening the drawbridge. The heads insinuated that there is something in this enterprise for me, but what could it be? Anyway, I hate the heads they always try to outdo me with their Greek Chorus. They consider their ditties to be "Narrative Poetry". I hope you find mine to be superior to theirs, as I sense they will be singing to you soon. Read my poem again and digest it so you may see how glorious it is.

Heads' Chorus

for Piano

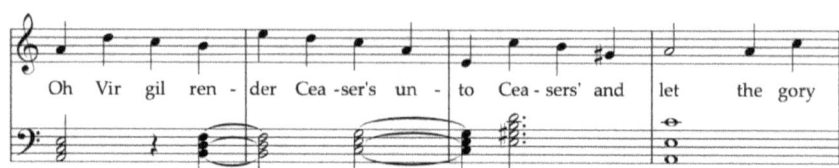

Oh Vir - gil ren - der Cea -ser's un - to Cea - sers' and let the gory

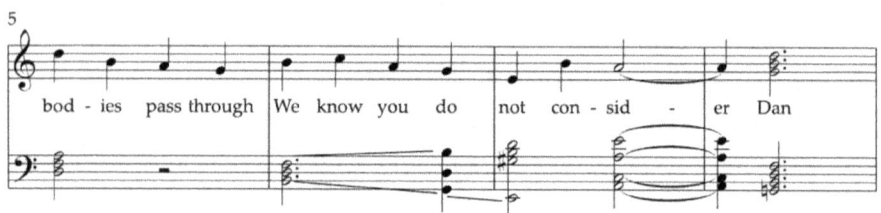

bod - ies pass through We know you do not con - sid - er Dan

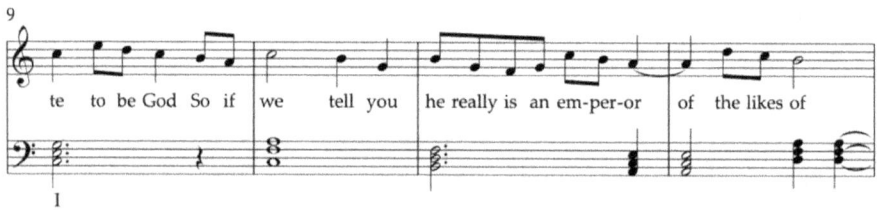

te to be God So if we tell you he really is an em-per-or of the likes of

you knew when you were a - live in Rome may - be you will

From the desk of Virgil – Poet and Warden of Old London Bridge
PURGATORY – TERRACE OF ENVY

Now let's get back to the happenings on Old London Bridge itself. I just delivered a telegram to a certain Sapia. In my opinion Sapia should be in Hell, for what she did in life, but I am not God, I am not Dante so who am I to judge? Sapia was happy when her nephew was killed defending her lands, as he was more popular than her in the kingdom. Sapia's nephew was never afraid to confront the enemy while she and her husband hid behind the safety of the ramparts. After she realized her error, of rejoicing in her nephew's death, she used her wealth to open a hospital in Sienna. A noble altruistic act in itself, yes, but when the forceps of guilt causes such an act to happen, it is just that - an act.

After I take the message that is to be sent as a telegram from under the door to Sepia's needle shop, I look up at the dilapidated sign with a needle painted on it. I think of Christ's way of saying that it would be easier for a camel to go through the eye of a needle than for a rich man to get into heaven. The wind blows and the wooden sign gives a creek on its rusty hinges as the owl hoots in the distance in the forest. How many executions do their big eyes witness?

Suddenly one of them flies over me with a mouse in its talons. I hear they swallow their prey whole, bones and everything only to vomit them in fluffy pellets which they leave in the open. Those birds, they are such Creon's and Henrys as they like the two men aforementioned both deny their victims a proper burial. The very idea is repulsive to me. I lean over the bridge and look down below. In the starless night the barge of bodies is illuminated by the hellfire over the sodomites. I look at the clothes of the victims. They range from the sackcloth of a monk to ermine-laced collar of the nobility. It seems that the King does not discriminate in terms of whom he kills. He leaves the hard work to Dante to sort out what level of Hell, Purgatory, or

Paradise they will go. The King is focused on one thing: Producing a male heir. May he never succeed. How can one respect the living if they desecrate the dead?

For what it's worth here is the poem below. I wish I had more time for revising but being a letter carrier as well as a warden is consuming all my time.

SAPIA

Sapia dances in the streets of Jerusalem,
like the rabbis do with the Torah. Her seat
of reason, her liver, has been eaten by an eagle.
It will not regrow. It is not immortal like
the gods who stole fire from Olympus

Oh, Prometheus when you stole fire
you lit up Sapia's heart to bet against
her own kin.

The gamble paid off in life.
Before her nephew's death
She had renounced God.

After she kissed The Almighty's feet
right before the Fates
cut her string of life.

Had she lived differently,
she could have kissed his lip
while still in her mortal body.

ST THOMAS BECKET CHAPEL
OLD LONDON BRIDGE

FROM: SAPIA– OWNER OF THE NEEDLE SHOP

TO: FORESE DONATI – OWNER OF THE PRETZEL SHOP

FORESE - STOP - I HEAR YOUR SISTER HAS BEEN
ELECTED TO PARLIAMENT. THE ONE WHOM YOU
FORCED OUT OF THE CONVENT - STOP PERHAPS YOU
CAN PETITION HER TO HELP - STOP - NONSENSICAL
PLANNING GOING ON DOWN BELOW - STOP - DO YOU
HEAR THE LETTERS READ BY THE HELLISH SOULS
BELOW, QUITE DISTURBING - STOP

SAPIA

From the desk of Virgil – Poet and Warden of Old London Bridge
PURGATORY – TERRACE OF GLUTTONY – Forese

Every sin in hell has its mirror in Purgatory and Gluttony is no exception. Unlike Ciacco, Forese will eventually get over his gluttony for profit as the owner of a brothel at the foot of the bridge. But until that day comes, he peddles it like a traveling salesman. The crude sign above his den of sin, an unclothed woman with a mouth agape and blindfolded. The sign is directly parallel to the upstairs window of one of the rooms. On hot stifling nights in the summer, through the window, the perverted groans can be heard.

I can't stand walking under this canopy of corrupt cries. Only when the sounds are masking the last words of those being executed in front of the Tower of London, do I welcome them. I have to say some of the last words of victims are worthy of being in one of Dante's Cantos. Too bad I have never had the time to record them. My only relationship with those who are executed is saying Masses for them when I get requests via letters from their families after they die . It is odd that no letters have come from the families of those of the bodies on the barge. Could they not need any? Could they be destined for Paradise?

Which leads me to my next point. Forse is unique on this bridge for he is the only one who has any contact with Parliament– his sister is there. Not only is his sister in Paradise for dedicating her life to God, but Forese is here in purgatory for gluttony. In my opinion his sentence should be extended, as it was he who dragged Piccarda out of her convent and cut short her mortal life as a bride of Christ, a nun. I wonder if he knows anything about the status of the bodies and their fate. What do you think of my little ditty below?

FORESE

Eyes pushed so far back in your skull
making the letter "M." Any mother
including Mary would cry at your state.

Forese, your stomach's a hillock that many
will write about. Poet whose pen
dueled with Dante's, you forsook your wife.

You glutton–Do I now plant a flag of sorrow for her
on your belly or one of victory as you are nearly out
of Purgatory?

ST THOMAS BECKET CHAPEL
OLD LONDON BRIDGE

FROM: FORESE–OWNER OF THE PRETZEL SHOP

TO: SAPIA–OWNER OF THE NEEDLE SHOP

HOW IS YOUR SEWING GOING? - STOP - ARE YOU
SEWING VEILS OUT OF PENNACE FOR REVELLING IN
THE DEATH OF YOUR NEPHEW DUE TO ENVY? – STOP -
I DID NOT KNOW THAT PICCARDA, MY SISTER, HAS
BEEN ELECTED TO PARLIAMENT - STOP - I'LL
CONSIDER PETITIONING HER - STOP

FORESE

ST THOMAS BECKET CHAPEL
OLD LONDON BRIDGE

FROM: SAPIA - OWNER OF THE NEEDLE SHOP

TO: FORESE DONATI – OWNER OF THE PRETZEL SHOP.

FORESE - STOP - I KNOW YOU HAVE A CRUSH ON ME -
STOP WE ALL KNOW VIA DANTE YOU ARE STUCK ON
THE BRIDGE BECAUSE YOU COULD NEVER SATISFY
YOUR WIFE – STOP - SO SATISFY ME AND WRITE YOUR
SISTER - STOP

SAPIA

From the desk of Virgil – Poet and Warden of Old London Bridge

The souls of Avarice are only silhouettes. They were so greatly in life seeking the treasure that lies in Pluto's domain, the bowels of the earth that they have been rendered to be unrecognizable. Poetry is imagery, so I will not write a formal poem about the soul that cannot be seen. Therefore, I have decided to leave you with a phrase that I think is quite appropriate. Money is the thing the souls of avarice desire above all else. The avaricious forget generosity; they hoard gold and make it their only means of living, in their greed depriving others of a better life. They are so focused on specie that they have become synonymous with it. All other aspects of their personality, their character, disappear. The phrase: "There are no strangers here, only friends we haven't met." suits them well.

February 16th
Anno Domini 1533

From:
Mr. Ciacco (Gluttonous Banker of Florence)
PO Box: Third Circle of Hell
Apt: Gluttony
666

To:
Mr. Avaricious Anonymous Soul (Avarice Greed)
PO Box: Fourth Circle
Apt: Greed
666

To Whom It May Concern:

　　I know that in life you took many bribes. Will you consider bribing Charon? We need your help getting these headless bodies under Old London Bridge.

Yours,

Ciacco

February 16th
Anno Domini 1533

From:
Mr. Avaricious Anonymous Soul (Avarice Greed)
PO Box: Fourth Circle
Apt: Greed
666

To:
Mr. Ciacco (Gluttonous Banker of Florence)
PO Box: Third Circle of Hell
Apt: Gluttony
666

Ciacco,

I was very disappointed that your letter was only three sentences. Due to my sins on Earth Dante may have rendered me unrecognizable - a featureless entity with only a silhouette - but my compassion in Hell should be noticed. Of course I will help.

Anonymous

From the desk of Virgil – Poet and Warden of Old London Bridge

This morning, a strong current almost carried away the letter I dropped off to Fillipo from the Bridge. That wrathful soul, he is a pathetic sight. He takes bites out of his own flesh which instantly heals only to repeat the practice. He dwells under the eighth arch – we call it the Bloody Arch as it always runs red with blood. Still, the trout swim in this water and swans traverse it. The birds' breasts are bloody and dappled like the stigmata. It is as if the animals have met their reckoning, only they are still alive! Is Fillipo jealous of them? I think so. Whenever a swan or trout swims close to the muddy mire, he tries to bite them and never succeeds. I wonder if the Parliamentarians even look out their south-facing widows down at the bloody river. I can't imagine they do, but I wish they would occasionally. Maybe then they would vote to block King Henry VIII from declaring war on France. Maybe they would do this if they saw Fillipo, the soul who is always at war with his own flesh and blood. He was wrathful in life and is in death

FILLIPO

Fillipo, you shod your horse with silver to earn
your nickname. Your steed trampled the
earth in anger. Now you bask under mud
unable to raise the hand against others
that you did on earth.

The weeping willow overhanging the Themes
cries. It recalls the notches you carved
denoting defeated opponents. Now it wallows
in vainglory missing being the herald
of your conquests.

February 17th
Anno Domini 1533

From:
Mr. Ciacco (Gluttonous Banker of Florence)
PO Box: Third Circle of Hell
Apt: Gluttony
666

To:
Mr. Fillipo Argenti (Wrathful Politician)
P.O. Box Fifth Circle of Hell
Apt: Wrath
666

Dear Fillipo,

   I was so glad that I spotted your fist out of water. I know it only happens once a month when the tides of Thames are extra low under the full moon. The time could not be more fortuitous. As you may know we are trying to help the headless bodies get this safe passage under Old London Bridge so they may be reunited with their heads. If Charon cannot be tempted to help with this perhaps you will.

Hope you'll join us.

Ciacco

February 19th
Anno Domini 1533

From:
Mr. Fillipo Argenti (Wrathful Politician)
P.O. Box Fifth Circle of Hell
Apt: Wrath
666

To:
Mr. Ciacco (Gluttonous Banker of Florence)
PO Box: Third Circle of Hell
Apt: Gluttony
666

Ciacco,

    Usually, I hate when my hand is above the water as that gives Charon a chance to slap it. He is so devious, that ferryman. Sure, I'll take you up on your offer, but it had better be in the next week or so. I wrote to Arnus a few weeks ago, the diviner of the stars. According to him, there is a huge storm brewing, one that might submerge my fist for over a month!

Kind regards,

Fillipo

From the desk of Virgil – Poet and Warden of Old London Bridge
HELL – THE HERETICS (SIXTH CIRCLE)

Imagine living in a fiery sarcophagus for eternity. This is the lot Dante assigned to the heretics, such as Lord Uberti, who subscribed to the notion that the soul dies with the body. Lord Uberti has set his shop for wallowing in his fire, just to the right of the mechanism for raising the drawbridge. It is as if he hopes that when it opens the water will run into his sarcophagus and momentarily cool him off. This has not happened yet, and I don't think it ever will. I remember once when Lord Uberti tried to move his sarcophagus closer to the drawbridge (when it was still made of wood) and he started a fire. The bridge burned, and we choked on smoke, but somehow the structure still stood. I think this is because it would have been heresy for Purgatory to fall into Hell.

My small cot is right above Uberti's sarcophagus. In the winter sin warms my old bones reminding me that I am just the bridge, Purgatory's custodian. Reminding me that I am condemned to limbo as I lived before Christ and never accepted him. Sometimes in the dead of winter I leave my bed and kneel down before the stained-glass window of Christ. I see how his crown of thorns contrasts with mine of laurel leaves, how his tunic is different from my toga, his hands stuck with nails in them against mine which grasps a quill. How can such a miserable man have entranced millions? Then shivering I return to my bed. When I again feel the warmth from Uberti's burning sarcophagus I recall how I did not have the opportunity buy into Jesus, and thus I am not saved. Remember, reader, Christ did had not existed during my lifetime. But enough wallowing in self-pity. Let me write instead.

LORD UBERTI

The leash on your soul is very taught.
You kept it in the rotting vessel of your body.
A simple mask possessed your simple mind –
retracted the pleasures of Paradise.

You kept your soul in the rotting vessel of the body.
The solace of babes and the old alike–
You retracted the pleasures of Paradise
by saying it dies. Now in a grave you live after death.

The soul, the solace of babes and the old alike–
taken from them like a pacifier or morphine–
You withheld it the pleasures of Paradise,
denied it emancipation.

Taken from them like a pacifier or morphine.
The soul's leash never ends for all but you.
You denied it emancipation.
A simple mask possessed your simple mind.

February 19th
Anno Domini 1533

From:
Mr. Arnus (Diviner of the Stars)
PO Box: Eighth Circle of Hell
Apt: Fraud
666

To:
Lord Farinata Degli Uberti (Heretic)
PO Box: Third Circle of Hell
Apt: Heresy
666

My Dear Lord,

You would dare speak against King Henry, let alone God himself? Such an act would be heretical, but then again, I suppose that is your nature. So, given that you are a heretic, can we count on you to out speak against those on Old London Bridge. Do you hear the heads at night crying for their bodies on the barge, or is your watery grave too deep? I'm looking forward to your response. If you join us, I will make sure you are exhumed from the coffin of yours quickly and painlessly.

With gratitude,

Arnus

February 21st
Anno Domini 1533

From:
Lord Farinata Degli Uberti (Heretic)
PO Box: Third Circle of Hell
Apt: Heresy
666

To:
Mr. Arnus (Diviner of the Stars)
PO Box: Eighth Circle of Hell
Apt: Fraud
666

Arnus,

    So good to hear from you! Of course I will join you! I am so glad that my epitaph has not worn off and that people and souls remember me! One question, or perhaps two: how are you going to read this letter if your head is up your ass, and how did you write it if your head is there too?

Lord Farinata degli Uberti

February 23rd
Anno Domini 1533

From:
Mr. Arnus (Diviner of the Stars)
PO Box: Eighth Circle of Hell
Apt: Fraud
666

To:
Lord Farinata Degli Uberti (Heretic)
PO Box: Third Circle of Hell
Apt: Heresy
666

My Lord,

The questions you ask! If you must know, I have learned to defecate letters around my mouth onto paper. What you are holding is ink made of shit. You must be so mortified even from beyond the grave that you want to burn this and the other letter I sent you.

Arnus

**From the desk of Virgil – Poet and Warden of Old London Bridge
PURGATORY – TERRACE OF LUST – Guido Guinizzelli**

If Ciacco loves the brothel for the money it produces, Guido Guinzzelli loves it for the pleasure the women give him. The brothel is right above the arch under which Francesca chases Paolo in the hellish river Themes. I've never been inside it, but I hear the straw mattress upon which the fornication takes place teems with lice and that rats scurry in every room, a grotesque audience watching a grotesque act, an act that could be so loving that has become perverted.

Guido himself is a sight to behold. Blind from syphilis he hires a guide to guide him to the brothel and escort him to the woman of his choice. His face is pockmarked. Every time Guido exits the brothel a new crater graces his face, a scarlet letter of his debauchery.

Once I caught Guido red-handed trying to steal from the tax box. He nearly made off with a dozen shillings. Only his tripping over a candle stick allowed me to catch him and wrestle him to the ground and take his money. Now penniless he begs for alms to feed his appetite for the flesh. How he sees the craters on his face as a testament to his manhood is a mystery to me. Perhaps he thinks when he is purified of his sin, and crosses into parliament that he will be able to use charisma and not looks to keep his constituents happy, allowing him more terms in his seat. My work about Lust in Hell was fairly long and I don't want to bore you, so here is its version for Purgatory. I think it is succinct and fits well on the page. I think that the format is pleasing to the eye. Oh, I should mention that Guido was a poet of love poems who influenced Dante. One would think that if Dante is a merciful God that he would have raised him to Parliament, to Paradise. But no, Guido is in Purgatory. As they say, The Lord works in mysterious ways.

GUINIZZELLI

Dante's mentor led him in pure verse.
Down footpaths of tercets, over hilly
dactyls, and through fields of quatrains.
Guido caused his protegee to nearly become
tongue-tied in describing altruistic love.
But Dante did not follow in the hunt.
He did not pursue the dappled hind
that got caught in Lust's snare.

ST THOMAS BECKET CHAPEL
OLD LONDON BRIDGE

FROM: HIS HOLINESS THE HOLY FATHER POPE
ADRIAN V

TO: GUIDO GUINIZZELLI (OWNER OF THE BROTHEL)

SIGNORE GUINIZELLI I AM SEEKING SHELTER IN
YOUR HOUSE OF ILL REPUTE -STOP - I THINK I NOW
HAVE ENOUGH MONEY TO BED ANY WHORE IN YOUR
BROTHEL - STOP - YOU MUST KNOW OF THE BODIES
ON THE BARGE - STOP I DON'T WANT TO BE
DISCOVERED - STOP - I DON'T WANT TO HAVE TO
CONSECRATE SACRED GROUND FOR THEIR BURIAL -
STOP

POPE ADRIAN V

From the desk of Virgil – Poet and Warden of Old London Bridge
PURGATORY – TERRACE OF AVARICE

Pope Adrian is in the most unique position on the bridge. Not only is he the ghost of the Holy Father, but he is in the middle of the bridge in a hole, his face right under the arch looking at his anonymous counterparts who are in Hell for the same sin. Every day I hear the Pope counting what he thinks are coins in the anonymous soul's, the avaricious soul's begging bowl, his "alms" bowl. It really is quite comical, that the avaricious soul has a begging bowl. What is he trying to be some Buddhist monk, is he trying to feign holiness. Does he think that I am duped into thinking he is praying for me and thus I should subsidize him financially. Every time he almost completes his calculations the bowls are dropped and coins scatter. After they are picked up the Pope must start counting again.

If only he had counted his sheep who needed saving while in life, instead of his money. The sight of the Pope's legs and feet sticking up in the middle of the bridge is quite a comical sight. We say that he is upside down in the stocks. I have always wanted to see his vestments as I have heard they are beautiful. I hear his triregnum is embroidered with the finest silk that comes from a far-off undiscovered land, and that it is set with gold lace. Perhaps when I one day open the door by the waterline of the Thames that is there for emergencies, I can gaze upon the greedy Pope. Until then I will have to content myself hearing him count the coins he wants to pilfer and then have to start again when the anonymous avaricious souls drop them. I must admit the curses between his counting are quite amusing and even make me, a pagan man of the cloth, blush.

I entertained the idea of "passing over" Adrian. I debated whether a man of such high office who has such a foul mouth deserves a poem. But to be consistent I wrote one.

POPE ADRIAN V

He who cannot see out of greed cannot count his money accurately.
He who cannot count his money cannot see his debts.
The chair of St. Peter where Adrian once sat was so close to God.
It was higher than the terrace of Purgatory a terrace of great
fearful heights– It could have been his steppingstone to Paradise.
Blind in life Adrian sees his folly in death.

ST THOMAS BECKET CHAPEL
OLD LONDON BRIDGE

FROM: GUIDO GUINIZZELLI

TO: HIS HOLINESS THE HOLY FATHER POPE ADRIAN V

YOUR HOLINESS – STOP - I AM ALWAYS READY TO
ACCEPT ANY CUSTOMER – STOP - HOWEVER I HAVE
RUN OUT OF WOMEN - STOP - ACCORDING TO YOUR
LAST COMMUNICATION YOU STATETHAT YOU ARE
OPPOSED TO THE ACT OF CHARITY OF OPENING THE
BRIDGE–IS THIS REALLY TRUE-STOP

GUIDO GUINIZZELLI

ST THOMAS BECKET CHAPEL
OLD LONDON BRIDGE

FROM: HIS HOLINESS THE HOLY FATHER POPE
ADRIAN V

TO: GUIDO GUINIZZELLI

GUIDO - STOP OF COURSE I AM OPPOSED - STOP I
WOULD HAVE THOUGHT MY LAST TELEGRAM MADE
THAT CLEAR - STOP - NOW YOU HAVE FORCED ME TO
SPEND A SHILLING ON THIS ONE - STOP

POPE ADRIAN V

From the desk of Virgil – Poet and Warden of Old London Bridge
HELL– THE VIOLENT (SEVENTH CIRCLE Cont'd)

Arch twelve is the thinnest of all. It is about a foot thinner than the others, and it is courtesy Alexander the Great. While I do not have to worry about the arch's discrepancies affecting the soundness of the bridge, for now, eventually it will be a problem I have to attend to. I am sure you know the saying "The Glory that was Greece and the Grandeur that was Rome." Well, my friends, Alexander has lost his glory and now lives in the boggy part of the river. His chariot wheels have great difficulty turning in the mire, but he still manages to charge the bridge. He thinks this is the enemy he fought in life. Every time Alexander charges, he hurts his arm when he hits the stone.

I must say that Alexander is very focused. Somehow, he is oblivious to the curses he receives from both the other hellish souls and those on the bridge as he shakes its foundations. You know the drill. Here is my poem below:

ALEXANDER THE GREAT

Violence was always at the doorstep of Alexander's mind.
In life, it was his loyal dog–
It was a dog that he rationalized.
Alexander made violence good in his mind.
He used the idea Pavlov's conditioning
For Alexander this conditioning was prayer.
He prayed to the gods before battle.
To him this made his enterprise of slaughter just.

February 25th
Anno Domini 1533

From:
Mr. Arnus (Diviner of the Stars)
PO Box: Eighth Circle of Hell
Apt: Fraud
666

To:
Alexander the Great (Violence Against Others)
PO Box: Seventh Circle of Hell
Apt: Violence
666

Alexander,

You and your armies are needed to block the bridge. Please return from whatever mythological battle you are fighting right away. Time is of the essence. Should Virgil raise the bridge we are doomed. I cannot believe that no one is on to the fact that I want to block the headless from crossing into Purgatory. I would have thought that since I have my head up my ass, since I see things backwards, it would have been a "dead giveaway," that I am against anything that could be remotely "good."

Very Truly Yours,

Arnus

February 27th
Anno Domini 1533

From:
Alexander the Great (Violence Against Others)
PO Box: Seventh Circle of Hell
Apt: Violence
666

To:
Mr. Arnus (Diviner of the Stars)
PO Box: Eighth Circle of Hell
Apt: Fraud
666

Arnus,

    Your letter annoys me. Don't you think that I am already aware of this barge of headless bodies, these so-called martyrs that were executed in The Tower of London? My punishment in Hell is to be in a river of boiled blood, and I must say the blood of these "martyrs" which has flowed into the river makes it much hotter because they must have been so pure in life. As soon as my men and I felt the heat we at once called off our other campaigns. If I need to, I will confront Virgil myself. By Almighty Zeus I swear this.

Alex

From:
Mr. Arnus (Diviner of the Stars)
PO Box: Eighth Circle of Hell
Apt: Fraud
666

To:
Mr. Ciacco (Gluttonous Banker of Florence)
PO Box: Third Circle of Hell
Apt: Gluttony
666

My Dear Ciacco,

     I have contacted all the souls you requested me to and I trust you have done the same. I suggest that we confront the souls on Old London Bridge on the Ides of March. Virgil and his tenants will never suspect that Hell would betray Purgatory (how could it?) and it will give us sufficient time to prepare. Thoughts?

Arnus

March 1st
Anno Domini 1533

From:
Mr. Ciacco (Gluttonous Banker of Florence)
PO Box: Third Circle of Hell
Apt: Gluttony
666

To:
Mr. Arnus (Diviner of the Stars)
PO Box: Eighth Circle of Hell
Apt: Fraud
666

Arnus,

I have to say that I am very impressed that we got this done in under a month. The Ides of March sounds perfect. Do you think that either Francesca or Brunetto were able to convince Charon to help us? I think that Virgil is a reasonable man and that he will try to help us. As for the others on that accursed bridge, who knows?

Ciacco

From the desk of Virgil – Poet and Warden of Old London Bridge
PURGATORY –TERRACE OF AVARICE

Next to Adrian dwells Hugh Capet. He is in the stocks too, for lusting after earthly power. The stocks where Hugh is confined to are "normal." They do not cause him to face downward in a hole. Being next to Adrian, Hugh is forced to smell the pope's feet. Hugh tickles them in return, a small recompense. I find it so fitting that the king of the temporal world and that of the spiritual are doing penance together. Yes, they disrupt the carts that pay tolls to cross Old London Bridge, and were Hugh and the Pope not there, I could earn more as the warden. But such is life.

HUGH'S LESSON

The lay person in Purgatory fares no better than the Pope.
The temporal chair is no better seat than the Throne of St Peter.
So, King Hugh learns when he faces the Pope's feet
and waits – waits for God's mercy.

ST THOMAS BECKET CHAPEL
OLD LONDON BRIDGE

FROM: GUIDO GUINIZELLI

TO: HUGH CAPET (OWNER OF THE HOUSE OF
WRITING IMPLEMENTS)

      YOUR MAJESTY - STOP - I GAVE THE WARDEN
VIRGIL AN EXTRA TRIP BY WRITING YOU - STOP -
POPE ADRIAN THE SPIRITUAL MASTER ON THIS
BRIDGE GAVE ME A PIECE OF HIS MIND - STOP -
MAYBE YOU CAN BE MORE GENTLE WITH ME - STOP -
INSTEAD OF CALCULATING YOUR EARNINGS PLEASE
CALCULATE WHETHER WE CAN HOLD OFF THIS
BARGE BELOW AT ALL THE TIDES - STOP - THE
THAMES IS UNPREDICTABLE AT THIS TIME OF YEAR -
STOP

GUIDO GUINIZZELLI

ST THOMAS BECKET CHAPEL
OLD LONDON BRIDGE

FROM: HUGH CAPET (OWNER OF THE HOUSE OF
WRITING IMPLEMENTS)

TO: GUIDO GUINIZELLI

GUIDO – STOP - I AM DISSAPOINTED THAT YOU
ARE SO BEHIND THE TIMES - STOP - I WOULD HAVE
THOUGHT THAT WITH KING HENRY VIII'S
DISSOLVING OF THE CHURCH AND MAKING HIMSELF
THE HEAD AS A TEMPORAL RULER THAT YOU WOULD
HAVE CONTACTED ME FIRST AND NOT THAT
POMPOUS POPE ADRIAN V – STOP - I WAS ACTUALLY
CALCULATING THE PROFITS THAT YOUR WHORES
MADE FOR YOU AS REQUESTED STOP BUT I AM HAPPY
TO GO ON AND CALCUATE HOW TO STOP THIS BOAT
AS IT IS IMPERATIVE THAT WE DO SO - STOP

HUGH CAPET

From the desk of Virgil – Poet and Warden of Old London Bridge
BRIDGE TO PARADISE

These heads are starting to drive me crazy. Yes, I pray, but I
pray to pagan gods. So how
can there be a place for me in Heaven? Who is this Dante, what
can he offer me? The souls
below are mad and are in troubled waters. Paradise, Parliament,
needs to end this; they need to
pass an act allowing the bodies passage under the bridge. No one
seems to understand that I cannot
do anything until such an act is passed, or, if I did do something,
such an action would be
unprecedented.

PLEA TO PARLIAMENT

Simon and Garfunkel's voices are hoarse.
Scratchy like Brillo they clear their throats.
Old London Bridge is indeed over troubled
waters. There is nothing to "lay down" but
the gauntlet. This madness, it can only be
stopped by an act of Parliament.
To parley means to speak, not to sing.

FROM: FORESE OWNER OF THE PRETZEL SHOP

TO: PARLIAMENT HOUSE OF COMMONS CHAMBER –
PICCARDA DONATI –MEMBER OF PARLIAMENT
DISTRICT OF THE MOON SPHERE

DEAR SISTER – STOP - I DOUBT YOU ARE GOING TO
RESPOND - STOP - I KNOW YOU TOLD ME TO NEVER
WRITE TO YOU AGAIN AFTER I ALLEGEDLY ASSISTED
IN FORCING YOU OUT OF THAT WRETCHED CONVENT
– STOP - I'LL HAVE YOU KNOW IT WAS OUR BROTHER
CORSO'S SOLE DOING I HAD NOTHING TO DO WITH
THIS MISFORTUNE OF YOURS – STOP - HOWEVER I
MUST TELL YOU THAT THE HELLISH SOULS IN THE
THAMES ARE TRYING TO ALLOW A BARGE FULL OF
SAINTLY SOULS THROUGH – STOP - SHOULD THEY
GET TO PARLIAMENT - STOP THEY MAY UPSET THE
MAJORITY YOU HOLD - STOP

FORESE

From the desk of Virgil – Poet and Warden of Old London Bridge
PARADISE–SPHERE OF THE MOON

Now we come to things I have only heard about. I have
never been to Parliament, known as Paradise. But sometimes the
debates get so heated that people shout, and I can hear them. I
know you must think that this is most undignified behavior for
those who sit near the throne of God, the Prime Minister. But this
is how it is.

My favorite inhabitant of Paradise is none other than
Forese's sister, Piccarda. She represents the district of the moon.
Sometimes when I look up at the sky and see the moon waxing
and waning, I wonder if it is a symbol of how her constituents feel
about her during the month. Of course, I know that this is not an
accurate way to measure feelings but still it is fun to think of
symbolism. Taken out a convent against her will, she is assigned to
the lowest level of Paradise, thinking that she should have died
instead of forsaking God.

On another note, the way in which the Parliamentarians
communicate is most strange. It is so impersonal. But I must
divulge that lately I have been reading a flurry of these emails, and
it is not because of the Ravens, it is because Arnus – that misfit –
has apparently hacked into the computers and is giving them to
me. He sure is going to have a lot to confess. I wonder if he ever
will. What does he have to lose? I am padding my straw mattress
with these emails. I hope they act as a counterweight to the heat I
feel from the Uberti's open tomb. I hope that they absorb some of
it so I do not sweat so much at night.

I've also put some of them in my pillowcase. Sometimes as
my head rests on them I dream of Paradise and being pure, only
to awake to the cruel reality of my lot. There is no debate where I
stand in life, but like the Parliamentarians, I will never lose my
seat. I will always be the

Warden of Old London Bridge. And even if I were to be "pushed out" somehow, I'll always be a poet. Here is my attempt to describe the saintly figures of Parliament, of Paradise.

PICCARDA DONATI

Jacob looked upon his first wife
and found Leah when had wanted
Rachel. He married Rachel and then neglected Leah.
So, the mirror of circumstance matches
with Piccarda Donati.

A pious nun
Forced out of her convent she still abandoned her vows.
The devout see her flaws wax and wane with the nights.
Unable to pin her down, unable to get her to confess her
shortcomings
their homage is inconsistent.
The faithful, they look for other more concrete guides of virtue
beyond the horizon.

To: Justinian@parliament.gov; CMartel@parliament.gov ;
STThomasAquinas@parliamnet.gov ;
Cacciguida@parliament.gov ; Constantine@parliament.gov ;
STBenedict@parliament.gov ; AngelChoir@parliament.gov;
STPeter@parliamnet.gov

SUBJECT HEADING: My brother Forese's Warning

My esteemed colleagues,

    It has come to my attention via a telegram sent by my
brother that bodies of martyrs executed by the King seek passage
under Old London Bridge. Does anyone know their political
persuasions? Did anyone interact with them before their demise?
Were they given access to the Parliament Chaplain? My concern is
that if these souls come to Paradise and form a party that they will
scuttle our plan to oust the Prime Minister, to oust God, Dante.
Please share with me your thoughts.

Your Honorable Friend,

Piccarda Donati
(MP District of the Moon)

ST THOMAS BECKET CHAPEL
OLD LONDON BRIDGE

FROM: PICCARDA DONATI MP OF SPHERE OF THE
MOON

TO: FORESE DONATI– OWNER OF THE PRETZEL SHOP

FORESE - STOP HOW DID YOU FIND ME - STOP NOW I
KNOW THAT YOU ONLY CONTACT ME WHEN YOU
WANT SOMETHING – STOP - YOU COULD HAVE AT
LEAST APOLOGIZED TO ME FOR THROWING ME OUT
OF MY CONVENT – STOP - ALTHOUGH I MUST ADMIT
THAT IN RETROSPECT THIS IS PROBABLY WHY DANTE
ASSIGNED ME TO PARADISE - STOP WHAT TERRACE
OF PURGATORY ARE YOU ON ANYWAY - STOP I
ASSUME IT IS LUST GIVEN WHERE YOU HAVE SET UP
SHOP - STOP - DO YOU KNOW THE POLITICAL
PERSUATIONS OF THESE BODIES THAT YOU SPEAK OF
OR BETTER YET THEIR HEADS WHICH HANG ON
LONDON BRIDGE - STOP

YOUR SISTER,

PICCARDA

From the desk of Virgil – Poet, and Warden of Old London Bridge
PURGATORY –TERRACE OF THE EXCOMMUNICATE

Now we come to one of the lowest levels of Purgatory that I must describe–that of the excommunicate. King Manfred was thrown out of the church by the Pope, for accepting that his lands to be ruled by another rather than coming under the jurisdiction of the Papacy. Still, he repented before his death and so he is here on Old London Bridge and not down in the Thames with the Hellish souls.

He owns no shop and has nowhere to sleep, save an old lean-too that he has created near the center of the bridge. Perhaps you wonder why he does not have a tent or something with four walls to keep out the cold. Well, the answer to that is simple, his vocation precludes him from that. Manfred's job is to empty the chamber pots for all the souls on Old London Bridge. He tells me that those from the brothels smell the worst, and I can only imagine why. Were he to have a dwelling with four walls and proper ceiling the stench would be too much to bear. The lean-to provides some much-needed ventilation.

I once considered inviting him to stay in the chapel so as to shield him from the rain, but had second thoughts as the stench of human waste would not be fitting in a house of God. Every day at dawn he wanders like a Sadhu, with matted hair, over the bridge collecting the waste. His only amusement is that he gets to choose from which arch he drops the waste. Every day the hellish souls make empty promises hoping that Manfred will spare them the contents of the pots from landing on their heads. I wonder whom he will choose today to grace with a crown of excrement.

KING MANFRED

Twice thrown out of God's house
Manfred, King of Sicily recalled
his soul back into the fold of Christ's sheep.

His body in unconsecrated ground–
and thrown into a river–
He fishes for it by night off Old
London Bridge. And when he comes
up empty he curses and throws the
excrement he is condemned to collect
into the Thames.

ST THOMAS BECKET CHAPEL
OLD LONDON BRIDGE

FROM: MANFRED –EX KING OF SICILY REMOVER OF
THE CHAMBER POTS ON LONDON BRIDGE

TO: FORESE DONATI–OWNER OF THE PRETZEL SHOP

FORESE – STOP - ALLOW ME TO CONGRATULATE YOU
ON REACHING YOUR SISTER – STOP - WE ARE GOING
TO NEED HER AID – STOP - BY THE WAY DID SHE TELL
YOU THAT SHE AND ALL THE OTHER SOULS IN QUOTE
PARADISE END QUOTE ARE PLOTTING AGAINST THE
PRIME MINISTER AKA GOD. DO YOU KNOW WHY –
STOP - THEY ALL THINK THAT THEY ARE GOD
THEMSELVES - STOP - OF COURSE YOU ARE GOING TO
ASK ME HOW I KNOW THIS - STOP - I HACKED INTO
YOUR SISTER'S COMPUTER WITH THE AID OF ARNUS -
STOP - I ALSO INFORMED HER THAT I DO BELIEVE IT IS
IN HER AND THE OTHER SOULS IN PARLIAMENTS'
INTERESTS TO RECEIVE THOSE OF THE BODIES ON
THE BARGE - STOP - WHY DID I DO THIS I HAVE
NOTHING TO LOSE – STOP - I AM ON THE LOWEST
RUNG OF PURGATORY, THE EXCOMMUNICATED - STOP

REGARDS,

MANFRED

Heads' Chorus

for Piano

2

21
tells our sage that Dan-te has been wri - ting

25
in the first in-fer-no all the souls are im-mor-tal- ized in print

29
Damned for all e-ter-nity in the hands of rea-ders as of those in Hell Ar-nus tried to

34
get old Vir gil To write Dan - te to im-plore God to stop His

38
ho - ly work but Vir - gil re - buffs Him

ST THOMAS BECKET CHAPEL
OLD LONDON BRIDGE

FROM: FORESE OWNER OF THE PRETZEL SHOP

TO: MANFRED–EX KING OF SICILY REMOVER OF THE
CHAMBER POTS ON LONDON BRIDGE

MANFRED STOP - I AM OVERJOYED AT YOUR SUCCESS
ON THE ONE HAND BUT AM MIFFED ON THE OTHER
STOP ALTHOUGH I FEEL RELIEVED TO KNOW THAT
MY SISTER WILL NOW HELP US TO END THIS QUOTE
EXPEDITION END QUOTE OF THAT BARGE – STOP - TO
SHOW MY GRATITUDE I WILL WRITE TO VIRGIL
ASKING HIM TO GIVE YOU A NEW ASSIGNMENT
OTHER THAN EMPTYING CHAMBER POTS – STOP - BY
THE WAY THE ONES IN MY BROTHEL ARE FULL WE
HAD A VERY BUSY NIGHT LAST NIGHT CAN YOU
EMPTY THEM - STOP

FORESE

From the desk of Virgil – Poet, and Warden of Old London Bridge
PURGATORY –TERRACE OF THOSE WHO DIED
VIOLENTLY

A healthy soul can only live in a healthy body. The question is: can a sick body die in a healthy soul? For Iacopo de Cassero was wounded by his enemies. Rather than die in their presence on the field he tried to save himself by taking refuge in a swamp. He died there and desecrated his own mortal flesh.

Now to save face, Iacapo is a blacksmith, the soot from his shop always masking his mangled face and body. He smelts the finest horseshoes, symbols of status of the well to do who ride their horses over the bridge. He also repairs wagon wheels and tongs when carts carrying goods need them replaced. When he does not get enough commissions, he makes spare candlesticks for my chapel. Most are of bronze, but some are of silver and a few even of gold. The poor man fears his face being discovered and is ashamed. I wonder if he knows that according to what I have heard, the Christian God loves all no matter how they look. But enough of me. Back to my poetry below.

IACOPO

Iacopo del Cassero
did not take care of his
body. When wounded, he
ran and bled to death
in a swamp.

He rejected Plato's
dictum about the body and the soul,
but accepted God's
He repented at the
last second.

ST THOMAS BECKET CHAPEL
OLD LONDON BRIDGE

FROM: IACOPO DEL CASSERO – MAKER OF
HORSESHOES

TO: VIRGIL - WARDEN OF OLD LONDON BRIDGE

I WARN YOU DO NOT HELP THESE HELLISH SOULS
DOWN BELOW – STOP - IF YOU DO I SWEAR THAT I
WILL ACT NOW AS I DIED VIOLENTLY – STOP - I DO
NOT WANT TO STIR UP TROUBLE BUT IT IS
IMPERATIVE THAT WE DO NOT ALLOW THE BARGE TO
PASS UNDER OLD LONDON BRIDGE - STOP - IF THEY
DO PASS AND GO TO PARADISE IT WILL BE AGAINST
NATURE AS WE SOULS IN PURGATORY SHOULD GO
FIRST - STOP - DO YOU REALLY WANT TO GO AGAINST
GOD'S PLAN BY LETTING THEM PASS - STOP

YOUR HUMBLE SERVENT

IACOPO DEL CASSERO

ST THOMAS BECKET CHAPEL
OLD LONDON BRIDGE

FROM: VIRGIL - WARDEN OF OLD LONDON BRIDGE

TO: IACOPO DEL CASSERO – MAKER OF HORSESHOES

IACOPO – STOP - DO NOT MAKE THREATS – STOP - I
ACKNOWLEDGE YOUR CONCERNS ABOUT THE
HELLISH SOULS AND WILL ATTEND TO THE MATTER
ACCORDINGLY - STOP

YOURS

VIRGIL

From the desk of Virgil – Poet and Warden of Old London Bridge

      I can smell a coup. This morning a raven dropped a communique in my lap. Those saved souls in Paradise, in Parliament, are planning to overthrow God, the Prime Minister. Then they intend to attack one another until one of them usurps the office of The Almighty. In the chapel kneeling by the altar, I read the communique again and again. Even when the sun rises, and I am nearly blinded by the light in the eastern window I read. A coup against God would earn the Parliamentarians a place in the lowest level of Hell, they would be in Satan's mouth along with Judas and Brutus. Do they realize this? They must. Maybe Arnus will get his wish after all. How strange the world is. Here are my thoughts about the matter in verse.

THE RABBIT HOLE

The rabbit hole becomes deeper. The snakes
of Paradise show that they are longer than those
of hell.

Two coups brew one just and one profane,
And neither are where you would expect.
Parliament has been sickened by Jerusalem,
It has conceived another Judas. Those in hell
have remorse. What could be more against the
divine formation of the Afterlife
There is a new order
for the afterlife and I am the hinge
on its door.

To: Justinian@parliament.gov; CMartel@parliament.gov ;
STThomasAquinas@parliamnet.gov ;
Cacciguida@parliament.gov ; Constantine@parliament.gov ;
STBenedict@parliament.gov ; AngelChoir@parliament.gov ;
STPeter@parliamnet.gov

SUBJECT HEADING: My account was hacked

My esteemed colleagues,

It appears that my account was hacked by someone on Old London Bridge. IT is looking into the problem.

Your Honorable Friend

Piccarda Donati

From the desk of Virgil - Poet and Warden of Old London Bridge

Now we come to the Parliamentarian of the sphere who opened Pandora's box when it comes to governing. Constantine the Great, the Roman Emperor who converted to Christianity, donated his temporal authority to the Pope. This would have been fine in theory had not his successors had an issue with this–including our current King Henry VIII, who has broken with Rome and made himself the head of the new Church of England. I find it fitting that he represents the sphere of Jupiter, his constituents, the nobility, and even some Dukes in France lands which Henry VIII rules.

Some nights in the summers when I am done counting the toll monies I like down on the bridge and look at the stars. Once I saw them alighted. I would always take this as a good omen. Perhaps the world is in sync and humanity will solve all its problems. Now they are aligned again for the coup. It seems that Constantine forgets that he put in place what he is trying to undo. They say that power corrupts and apparently it went to this Emperor's head. As always, I direct you to the eloquence of poetry.

CONSTANTINE

*The stud never looks over his shoulder. Always
focused on the task at hand while in the bridle
of pleasure, he never thinks of the consequences.*

*So happened to Emperor Constantine when he
embraced Christianity. That act alone did not
spell government's doom. It gave the law,
morals, a path on which to walk.*

*His donation of his temporal power
The church blurred all these. Now,
Those blinded by power wander
the path in confusion.*

To: Justinian@parliament.gov; CMartel@parliament.gov ;
STThomasAquinas@parliamnet.gov ;
Cacciguida@parliament.gov ; PDonati@parliament.gov ;
STBenedict@parliament.gov ; AngelChoir@parliament.gov;
STPeter@parliament.gov

SUBJECT HEADING: How can we strike?

How can we strike at God and continue our coup when
there is one going on at Old London Bridge? Piccarda is right;
these hellish souls have a chance to derail our ambitions. Who
would have thought that the souls of Hell would try to create a
new heavenly order when their ambitions on Earth failed. We
must write to Virgil immediately telling him not to assist these
souls as he is keeper of the Bridge. We must all sign it. Even
though we all know we intend to stab each other in the back when
the time comes, this is in our mutual interest.

 Emperor Constantine
(MP Sphere of Jupiter)

ST THOMAS BECKET CHAPEL
OLD LONDON BRIDGE

FROM: THE MEMBERS OF PARLIAMENT

TO: VIRGIL – WARDEN OF OLD LONDON BRIDGE

HONORABLE VIRGIL - STOP - HOW THE TABLES HAVE
TURNED – STOP - NEVER DID WE THINK WE WOULD
BE BESSECHING YOU – STOP - YOU HAVE ALWAYS
MADE SURE CARTS AND TRAFFIC ARE TAXED FOR
USE OF OLD LONDON BRIDGE - STOP - YOU ALWAYS
MADE SURE THE MONIES WERE DELIVERED ON TIME
– STOP - NOW WE COME TO YOU ASKING ANOTHER
FAVOR – STOP - THE BODIES MUST NOT BE ALLOWED
TO PASS UNDER OLD LONDON BRIDGE – STOP - WE
ARE IN THE PROCESS OF DELICATE NEGOTIATIONS
INCLUDING ONES THAT MAY ALLOW YOU TO FINALLY
PASS THROUGH PURGATORY AND NOT BE
CONDEMNED TO LIMBO IN HELL – STOP - THESE
SOULS EXECUTED BY THE KING ARE "HOLIER THAT
THOU" – STOP - SHOULD YOU ALLOW THEM TO PASS
AND SHOULD THEY GAIN THEIR SEATS IN
PARLIAMENT WHICH THEY ARE ALLOWED TO BY THE
VIRTUE OF BEING ADMITTED INTO PARADISE THEY
WILL TABLE [1] OUR MOTION WHICH WE HAVE RAISED
ON BEHALF OF YOU - STOP

THE MEMBERS OF PARLIAMENT

ST THOMAS BECKET CHAPEL
OLD LONDON BRIDGE

FROM: GUIDO GUINIZZELLI

TO: THE SOULS ON OLD LONDON BRIDGE

DEAR COMRADES – STOP - I HAVE MADE AN
EXECUTIVE DECISION – STOP - AS THE SOUL ON THE
LEDGE OF LUST THE ONE THAT IS CLOSEST TO GOD
THE LEDGE THAT IS SIN OF THE FLESH AND NOT THE
MIND – STOP - I HAVE DECIDED TO INVITE THE SOULS
OF HELL UP ONTO OLD LONDON BRIDGE TO SPEAK
WITH THEM - STOP

GUIDO GUINIZZELLI

Heads' Chorus

March 13th
Anno Domini 1533

From:

Mr. Arnus (Diviner of the Stars)

PO Box: Eighth Circle of Hell

Apt: Fraud

666

To:

Mr. Ciacco (Gluttonous Banker of Florence)

PO Box: Third Circle of Hell

Apt: Gluttony

666

Ciaccio!

God has smiled on me (or at least He did momentarily). I have good and bad news. The good news is that I was able to get my head out of my ass for fifteen minutes and speak with Charon to see if he will aid us in our endeavor with the barge. The bad news is that he will not. Even we were to offer him half of the coinage (which is above his normal charge) in our mouths that were placed under our tongues when we died to (the other half we would have to save as I am sure the souls in Purgatory will take no less than half to allow us to pass under the bridge) he will not take the bodies on his skiff.

Sincerely,

Arnus (who has his head back up his ass)

March 13th
Anno Domini 1533

From:
Mr. Ciacco (Gluttonous Banker of Florence)
PO Box: Third Circle of Hell
Apt: Gluttony
666

To:
Mr. Arnus (Diviner of the Stars)
PO Box: Eighth Circle of Hell
Apt: Fraud
666

Arnus,

    The real blessing was to be able to smell fresh air for the first time. Don't worry. I will write to Virgil demanding passage under the bridge for the barge. If he and his cronies refuse, we will have to take the bodies one by one on small skiffs under the bridge to Paradise, to Parliament
Wish me luck.

Ciacco

March 15th
Anno Domini 1533

From:
Mr. Ciacco (Gluttonous Banker of Florence)
PO Box: Third Circle of Hell
Apt: Gluttony
666

To:
Mr. Virgil (Dante's guide through Hell and Purgato
PO Box: Old London Bridge
Apt: ST Thomas Becket Chapel
777

Honorable Virgil,

It has been a month and half of communicating amongst ourselves that has allowed us to reach the resolution to write to you. Obviously, you have noticed the barge below with the souls with the virtuous bodies whose heads are on pikes on your bridge. We write to you requesting passage under your bridge. We are willing to pay a fee (the coins that were placed under our tongues to cross the River Styx at our deaths) for going under.

Yours,

Ciacco

ST THOMAS BECKET CHAPEL
OLD LONDON BRIDGE

FROM: VIRGIL - WARDEN OF OLD LONDON BRIDGE

TO: CIACCO - THE GUTTONESS ONE

CIACCIO – STOP - I AM IN RECEIPT OF YOUR LETTER
DATED THE IDES OF MARCH IN THE YEAR OF OUR
LORD 1533 – STOP - I HAVE A SPOT OF GOOD NEWS –
STOP - THE SOULS ON THIS HUMBLE CAUSEWAY
CALLED PURGAROY HAVE ASKED ME TO INVITE YOU
AND YOUR MOTLEY CREW UP SO WE CAN RESOLVE
OUR DIFFERENCES - STOP - MEET ME AT THE DOOR
BY THE WATERLINE TOMORROW AT NOON SHARP -
STOP - I WILL FINALLY BE ABLE TO SATISFY MY
CURIOSITY OF GAZING AT THE SOULS OF HELL FORM
THEIR LEVEL - STOP

VIRGIL

From the desk of Virgil – Poet and Warden of Old London Bridge

This morning a raven dropped a printout of an electronic letter on the bridge next to the chapel. The letter was bloodied. It must have been dropped on or have grazed the bloody grass near the Tower of London where all the executions take place. Another execution took place on the Tower green in front of The Tower of London this morning. I can see some chicken scratch on the back of the electronic letter; it looks like the tabulation of votes. The poor soul had begged Parliament to intervene, but none came to his aid fearing the wrath of the King. This letter was written by St. Benedict, the vicar of Saturn's district. Old Saturn, the god who ate his young. How fitting given that Parliament did the same to one of its own constituents.

I have watched many an execution. They always use the same bloodied block. The crescent moon in which the neck goes is not a one-size-fits all, and nor are the hearts of the victims. Yes, some are stoic, but some writhe when they are forced to lie on the block Then there is the factor of whether the condemned is a common criminal for whom and axe is used or member of the nobility who is executed with a sword. What an unholy Trinity to think about, and to think about such a thing is most unpleasant. So once again let me contemplate.

ST BENEDICT

Like the rings of the planet, the girdle
of the Benedictine Rule rounds
his adherent's waists. A choker
more firm than the one round
Cerberus' neck, it keeps the
Monks in line– A path
with which to live by.
Each generation
equaling Saturn's
revolution.

To: Justinian@parliament.gov; CMartel@parliament.gov ;
Cacciguida@parliament.gov ; PDonati@parliament.gov ;
STThomas@parliament.gov ; AngelChoir@parliament.gov
Constantine@parliament.gov; Constantine@parliament.gov;
STPeter@parilament.gov

SUBJECT HEADING: GOD IS WITH US

Honorable friends, God is with us! How dare you all be alarmed? I was in shock when I read the email from my honorable friend Constantine. It reeked of panic, the panic of some forsaken soul who had never found Christ. I have gotten word that the souls of Hell are on Old London Bridge with those of Purgatory trying to sort out their differences. By the time they do, years will have elapsed and those bodies, those wolves in sheep's clothing will have rotted. Now we can return to your original plan of overthrowing the Prime Minster, God, and then turning on each other.

ST. Benedict

From the desk of Virgil – Poet and Warden of Old London Bridge

When alive, I worshipped gods. I hear all these souls from Hell, Purgatory, and Paradise worshipped or cursed a single God. Maybe that is why they are so dysfunctional. The feuds in these mortal families match those of the Olympias. How have these people lived with this so-called monotheism? When there are many gods, you can serve many masters and you can sometimes even "shop divinities" to get the favor you want. Not so for these modern souls.

Yes, the trappings of the afterlife remains the same. There is still Charon, and the souls still pay their fare in specie when they cross under the bridge. There is still the Elysian Fields in the guise of Parliament. But everything else is so different. Even though I dwell on a bridge, the chasm between how I lived and believed in terms of what happens after death is too great for me to make sense of how the afterlife works in these times. What is their God like, if he is one, and how can this one be three in this thing called the Trinity? This math would even baffle Pythagoras.

THE EMPYAREN – DWELLING OF GOD

Beth–El – God's house.
Pharoah – Great house.
Beyond the stars dwells God.

In the foyer of heaven is a rose nurtured
by angelic bees on which the souls sing.
Such a simple image goes against the grain
of the theologians' minds. Their complex
theories and dictums of hierarchies fly in the face
of this simple scene. The scenes of the heart,
the opera glasses of heaven.

March 16th
Anno Domini 1533

From:
Office of the Prime Minister
10 Downing Street
London SW1A 2AB, UK

To:
State Parliament
Palace of Westminster
9748 Abington Street
London

Honorable Parliamentarians,

    I have just received a note from His Majesty King Henry VIII that he will dissolve Parliament once again if the bodies on the bridge are not permitted to pass under Old London Bridge within a fortnight. While I am well aware that I am not liked by any of you, all your power will be stripped if this happens. I suggest you table a motion to allow the bodies to pass under the causeway as soon as possible.

God,

The Prime Minister

March 20th
Anno Domini 1533

From:
Madam Francesca (Adulterous Maiden)
PO Box: First Circle of Hell
Apt: Lust
666

To:
Mr. Arnus (Diviner of the Stars)
PO Box: Eighth Circle of Hell
Apt: Fraud
666

Arnus,

　　Your ass hole smells better than some of these souls I have been with. I am surprised that Vigil gave us access to the causeway so willingly. They are selling us a bill of goods. Last night I fornicated with King David. He called me the Queen of Sheba. I did not know whether to take it as a complement or an insult. All he accomplished by fucking me is prolonging his time in Purgatory, or perhaps he is trying to distract me from our mission of focusing on getting that barge under London Bridge. We must get the souls under so they can take their places in Paradise. If we succeed, if we are the ones who do, God might have pity on us and allow us to be there too. What have your experiences been?

Francesca

March 21st
Anno Domini 1533

From:
Mr. Arnus (Diviner of the Stars)
PO Box: Eighth Circle of Hell
Apt: Fraud
666

To:
Madam Francesca (Adulterous Maiden)
PO Box: First Circle of Hell
Apt: Lust
666

Dearest Francesca,

    Happy Spring! Perhaps this year my head will finally be totally out of my ass for more than a day. I have been fraternizing with Fillipo Argenti at Bellacqua's. We are trying to refashion his instrument into a contraption to get my head out. So far, we have devised the gut harp strings that will be placed on hooks and pull my head out. We are now trying to fashion a spring of silver to keep it out.

Yours,

Arnus

From the desk of Virgil – Poet, and Warden of Old London Bridge

I have to get the bodies through soon as they are starting to rot. What a simple sentence.

What a disgusting image. Allow me this sugar-coating verse

RECKONING

When pleasure courts man's mind
morality gives like the reed in the windy
field.
Old London Bridge suspends
the heads forcing them to watch
Their bodies beginning to putrefy
the chorus of debauchery
crescendos over the Thames.
Winding its way to an angry ocean
of reckoning.

ST THOMAS BECKET CHAPEL
OLD LONDON BRIDGE

FROM: FORESE - OWNER OF THE PRETZEL SHOP

TO: PARLIAMENT HOUSE OF COMMONS CHAMBER –
PICCARDA DONATI –MEMBER OF PARLIAMENT
DISTRICT OF THE MOON SPHERE

SISTER YOU CAN NOW FOCUS ON BECOMING THE
PRIME MINISTER - STOP - YOU CAN BECOME GOD
BECOME DANTE – STOP - MY COHORTS AND ME SEEM
TO HAVE STOPPED THE HELLISH SOULS WITH THE
SINS OF INCONTINENCE – STOP - THEIR MORALS ARE
BLEEDING MUCH LIKE THE HEADLESS BODIES ON
THE BARGE THAT STILL LANGUISHES ON THE
THAMES – STOP - SUCCEED IN YOUR BACKSTABBING
AND WHEN YOU BECOME PRIME MINISTER BE SURE
THAT YOU DO NOT FORGET ME - STOP

FORESE

March 22nd
Anno Domini 1533

From:
Mr. Fillipo Argenti (Wrathful Politician)
P.O. Box Fifth Circle of Hell
Apt: Wrath
666

To:
Mr. Ciacco (Gluttonous Banker of Florence)
PO Box: Third Circle of Hell
Apt: Gluttony
666

Ciacco,

I understand that you and Arnus went with Manfred to a tavern to celebrate Arnus' head being extracted from his ass once and for all! It is most fitting that you would celebrate with Manfred, the excommunicate as Arnus head is now excommunicated from his body. I was wondering, do you perhaps take this as a sign that we should return to our original mission of getting the virtuous bodies that rest on the barge through under the bridge. All of us have been so drunk on debauchery that we have forgotten our mission.

Yours,

Fillipo

From the desk of Virgil – Poet and Warden of Old London Bridge

Now I know, as Shakespeare would say, "Something is
rotten in Denmark." Today the
Raven dropped another printout of an email that was corrupted
by a computer virus. This one is short and naked. It does not even
try to hide the nefarious intentions it speaks about. It is a
declaration of war against God, a second coup if you will, as I
read about the first one in the Christian Bible. Leave it to a former
crusader who represents Mars the God of war to hatch a plan like
this. If you look at this email, you will see it is riddled with errors,
a paradox to the clarity of the cruel scheme.

How can I write a tragic piece to match this? Well, here is my
attempt below.

CACCIAGUIDA

War is man's means to an end.
What is passed down
is told by the victors.

On the ramparts of Jerusalem,
The crusaders sing and drink mead.
They speak volumes of eulogies for their dead
not noticing the streets bloodied by Muslims and Jews.

Even the humble friar does not write elegies for
The slain. He forgot the crusade was for Jesus
who forgives all.

Like the general Cacciaguida the friar
denies Christ his victory–leaving mortal man
to interpret his sins without a confessor.

To: PDonati@parliament.gov

SUBJECT HEADING: Fuuuull Moon

Dear Piccardaaaaa,

T000nite is a full moon. You know I harbor affections for you. Let us team up and rule Heaven as king and queen.

L0000ve,

Cacciaguida
(MP of the Sphere of Mars)

From the desk of Virgil – Poet and Warden of Old London Bridge

Everyone wants to bask under the sun, except for me. The heads are becoming very putrid. They still sing dirges about wanting to be reunited with their bodies below. David yells at them. He has been trying to pass his time in Purgatory by forming them into a chorus, however they will not follow the notes of his harp. Today' s communique comes from St. Thomas who doubted Christ. Still, in his mercy Christ had the sun rise over him it appears. The last I heard he was reelected in a landslide by his district. A sense of unease overhangs the bridge like a dense moist fog. The Hellish souls appear to be tiring of the charade being put on by my tenants. I feel it is only a matter of time before all Hell breaks loose. No matter what happens though the sun will still set and rise just as surely as my pen will glide across the parchment.

ST THOMAS

Thomas, doctor of the Church put philosophy under
anesthesia. He sent it to dream with angels. Then
he woke the work of the Greeks up and had it drink
The Eucharist. Now it's the centurion guarding faith
The high cause which it marches in lockstep with.

To: Justinian@parliament.gov; CMartel@parliament.gov ;
Cacciguida@parliament.gov ; STBenedict@parliament.gov
AngelChoir@parliament.gov Constantine@parliament.gov;
Constantine@parliament.gov ; STPeter@parliament.gov

SUBJECT HEADING: A First Victory

My esteemed colleges,

Heaven has let its light shine down. Cacciguida, who fought in the crusades and is Dante's great-great-grandfather, has launched another one. With his mighty lance he took down one of our own–Piccarda. Let us continue to sharpen our knives until one of us confronts The Prime Minister, God, Dante, and assumes the premiership, and all the divinity that comes with it.

ST Thomas
(MP Sphere of the Sun)

PS: Isn't it sad that she fell for a simple computer virus?

ST THOMAS BECKET CHAPEL
OLD LONDON BRIDGE

FROM: MANFRED - EX-KING OF SICILY & CLEANER OF
THE CHAMBER POTS ON OLD LONDON BRIDGE

TO: SAPIA – OWNER OF THE NEEDLE SHOP

IT IS TRULY AS JESUS SAID EASIER TO HAVE A CAMEL
GO THROUGH THE EYE OF A NEEDLE THAN FOR A
RICHMAN GET INTO HEAVEN - STOP - THESE POOR
HELLISH SOULS THEY HAVE NOT KNOWN PLEASURES
FOR MILLENIA - STOP - WE HAVE TO KEEP THIS UP -
STOP - SOON THE BODIES ON THE BARGE WILL HAVE
DECOMPOSED AND THEN WE CAN SHOW THEM THE
CRUEL REALITY THAT THEIR ACTIONS IN LIFE, THIER
TURNING AWAY FROM GOD HAVE BROUGHT UPON
THEM - STOP

MANFRED
(THE EXCOMUNICATE)

ST THOMAS BECKET CHAPEL
OLD LONDON BRIDGE

FROM: KING DAVID (KEEPER OF THE HEADS)

TO: HIS HOLINESS THE HOLY FATHER POPE ADRIAN V

YOUR HOLINESS THE AVARICIOUS ONE - STOP I KNOW
THAT YOU DO NOT WANT TO HAVE TO CONSECRATE
ANY SACRED GROUND FOR THE BURIAL OF THE
BODIES ON THE BARGE AND YOU MAY GET YOUR
WISH IF THINGS KEEP GOING AS THEY ARE - STOP
BUT THIS BRINGS ANOTHER PROBLEM - STOP - THE
HEADS ARE STARTING TO ROT ON THEIR PIKES – STOP
- WHAT IS MORE THEY ARE STARTING TO SPEAK THEY
HAVE COUNSELED VIRGIL - STOP - THEY ARE TELLING
HIM THINGS ABOUT GOD ABOUT DANTE THAT IF HE
BELIEVES IF HE BUYS INTO WILL NOT BE IN OUR
INTEREST AS IT MAY DELAY OUR GETTING INTO
PARADISE - STOP

KING DAVID
(THE PRIDEFUL)

ST THOMAS BECKET CHAPEL
OLD LONDON BRIDGE

FROM: HIS HOLINESS THE HOLY FATHER POPE
ADRIAN V

TO: KING DAVID – KEEPER OF THE HEADS

RULER OF THE TEMPORAL WORLD - STOP - IT MAKES
ME FEEL SO GOOD THAT WE CAN WORK TOGETHER -
STOP - THAT BAFFOON IN HEAVEN THAT MP FOR THE
SPHERE OF JUPITER CONSTANTINE -STOP - THAT
BAFFOON WHO GAVE TEMPORAL POWER TO ME
WHAT WAS HE THINKING - STOP - I AM GLAD WE CAN
CEASE OUR INFIGHTING AND WORK TOGETHER -
STOP - OUR WORKING TOGETHER TO BLOCK THE
MALICIOUS HEADS WILL DOVETAIL AS NICELY AS DO
THE OLD AND NEW TESTAMENTS - STOP

CHEERS
ADRIAN V

RETURN TO SENDER

FROM: FORESE – OWNER OF THE PRETZEL SHOP

TO: PICCARDA DONATI–MEMBER OF PARLIAMENT
DISTRICT OF THE MOON SPHERE

SISTER YOU CAN NOW FOCUS ON BECOMING THE
PRIME MINISTER, ON BECOMING GOD, ON BECOMING
DANTE - STOP - MY COHORTS AND I SEEM TO HAVE
HALTED THE HELLISH SOULS WITH THE SINS OF
INCONTINENCE - STOP - THEIR MORAL ARE
BLEEDING MUCH LIKE THE HEADLESS BODIES ON
THE BARGE THAT STILL LANGUISHES ON THE
THAMES - STOP - NOW SUCCEED IN YOUR
BACKSTABBING AND WHEN YOU BECOME PRIME
MINISTER BE SURE THAT YOU DO NOT FORGET ME -
STOP

FORESE

ST THOMAS BECKET CHAPEL
OLD LONDON BRIDGE

FROM: FORESE - OWNER OF THE PRETZEL SHOP

TO: GUIDO GUINZELLI

THE MOANING OF YOUR WHORES IS GOING TO
SOUND LIKE SIGHS OF JOY AFTER YOU HEAR WHAT I
HAVE TO TELL YOU - STOP - MY TELEGRAM TO MY
SISTER PICCARDA HAS BEEN RETURNED OUR ONLY
AVENUE IN PARADISE IN PARLIAMENT HAS BEEN CUT
OFF - STOP - THIS ENTERTAINING OF YOURS HAD
BEST BE ABLE TO BE KEPT UP FOR AT LEAST THE
NEXT TWO WEEKS UNTIL THE BODIES ON THE BARGE
DECOMPOSE IS THIS POSSIBLE - STOP - IF THE BOIDES
DO GET INTO PARLIAMENT THEY WILL FORM A
VOTING BLOCK THAT WILL ENSURE THAT GOD THAT
DANTE CANNOT BE OVERTHROWN STOP THEN ALL
WILL BE LOST -STOP - THAT DANTE IS QUITE A POET -
STOP - HE WILL PUT OUR STATES OF PURGATORY INTO
PRINT - STOP - AND OUR SHAMEFUL LIVES WILL BE
LAID BARE FOR POSTERITY FOREVER - STOP

FORESE

ST THOMAS BECKET CHAPEL
OLD LONDON BRIDGE

FROM: GUIDO GUINZELLO

TO: FORESE OWNER OF THE PRETZEL SHOP

FORESE - STOP - YOU WORRY TOO MUCH - STOP - SO
WHAT IF OUR MOLE IS LOST IN PARLIAMENT -STOP -
IT'S NOT AS IF YOU WERE CLOSE TO HER - STOP - IN
FACT YOU ARE THE REASON WHY SHE IS NOT IN A
HIGHER SPHERE OF HEAVEN -STOP - YOU FORCED
HER OUT OF THE CONVENT - STOP

GUIDO GUINZELLI

From the desk of: Virgil–Poet, and Warden of Old London Bridge
PARADISE–SPEHRE OF THE STARS

Now I have received a copy of an electronic letter written by ST. Peter. A raven dropped it in a chamber pot. I got into an argument with Manfred who finally let me have it. Back in the chapel at the small desk beside the altar, I feel that I must "reconsecrate my hands" given the smell and filth. From what I read either King Henry has finally grown a conscience, or he simply wants the earthly remains of those he executed out of his sight, so he does not have to think of the murders he has committed. I look out the window; it is unseasonably warm today. The icicles on Christ's are hair melting, allowing me to see his face clearly The coup against his father is becoming all too apparent. The only thing that is crystal clear is that Henry continues to deny the authority of the Pope just as Peter denied Christ in the Garden of Gethsemane.

ST PETER

Two keys–one to heaven, and one to Earth.
Poor Peter never should have taken
Constantine up on his offer–
To be a spiritual and temporal ruler. The cylinders of the locks are
so different.

> *One is lubed and oil the other stiff and rusty.*
> *Sometimes their states change places.*
> *The pen of the Vatican is small*
> *the fields of the world are vast*
> *there is no denying this.*

Every morning the rooster crows waking the first pope up.
There is work to do. Souls must be saved. Even if you denied
God before assuming your office.

To: Justinian@parliament.gov; CMartel@parliament.gov ;
Cacciguida@parliament.gov ; STBenedict@parliament.gov
AngelChoir@parliament.gov Constantine@parliament.gov;
STThomas@parliament.gov

SUBJECT HEADING: If Only

     If only the King had not challenged the papacy, had not challenged me! This morning, I received a memo from the PM who has been in contact with the king. According to the Prime Minister, God, Dante if the bodies are not allowed to pass within a fortnight under Old London Bridge, he will dissolve Parliament. I am sure I am repeating what you already know. What are we to do?

ST Peter
MP of the Starry Sphere)

From the desk of Virgil – Poet and Warden of Old London Bridge
PARADISE –S PEHRE VENUS

Now I have a communique from the MP of the sphere of love. I always wondered how Charles Martel wound up with Venus. True ,he did turn back the Arabs from Europe when he defeated them. Perhaps it was his love for Christianity that made Dante put him in this sphere. I decided to take an afternoon stroll today; when I looked over the bridge, I noticed that the bodies have turned black and are decomposing quickly. When I pass David, the heads are hesitating to sing. All they talk about is hoping that they can rot as fast as the bodies below, for they cannot bear to be "alive" seeing their bodies in this condition.

Spring is coming and the ice on the Thames is breaking up. I can hear the water flowing faster. Soon, I will have to inspect the bridge to see what must be repaired. If the repairs are great, I may have to raise the tolls to cross it, but I am determined not to raise the tolls for those who pass under it. I respect the dead more than the living, and given that I do this, the haiku below is a vivid memorial to the Muslim dead that Charles left in his wake as he drove the Arabs out of Europe to save Christendom.

CHARLES MARTEL

The first poppy field
created in Islam's blood
Europe's great savior

To: STPeter@parilament.gov

SUBJECT HEADING: You've got everything upside down

Peter,

Firstly, thank God the virus is gone in our computers. Secondly, you have everything upside down. While it is to be expected as you met your demise on an upside down cross, I am still surprised at you. Usually your hands do not shake when you open heaven. You never doubt a soul who comes before you, yet now you cower before a King, Henry VIII who is still on Earth! Well, in retrospect I suppose this makes sense as well since you denied Christ three times in the Garden of Gethsemane because you feared mortal men. We still have ten days to take care of one another before we have to deal with the bodies. If I were Prime Minister now it would be so easy for me to stand up to the King.

Charles Martel
(MP of the Sphere of Venus)

To: CMartel@parliamnet.gov

SUBJECT HEADING: Is it true?

Charlie,

It must have been fortuitous that I was absent for the past two days. I hear there was a motion to gerrymander districts. Is it true that mine is being joined with St. Benedict's?

Saint Peter
(MP of the Starry Sphere)

To: STPeter@parilament.gov

SUBJECT HEADING: You are correct

Peter,

Yes, I called a motion with Piccarda gone. We had to divide her constituents, and since yours and Saint Benedict's are the least populous, we all agreed they should go with you. That part of the motion went over fine. But then all of sudden Constantine, in his brilliance, suggested that your districts be merged. Benedict was against it, but the motion was paused through even though the Prime Minister voted ???for it.??? Do you mean against. Now, do what you are paid to do; table a motion that says only one MP can serve your district. Get rid of Benedict! Get rid of him so we can continue our infighting until only one of us is left to challenge and finally overthrow God, overthrow Dante.

Charles Martel
(MP of the Sphere of Venus)

ST THOMAS BECKET CHAPEL
OLD LONDON BRIDGE

FROM: HIS HOLINESS THE HOLY FATHER POPE
ADRIAN V

TO: THE HEADS OF LONDON BRIDGE

HEADS OF THE BODIES OF THE BARGE - STOP - YOUR
QUIBBLING - STOP - YOUR BODIES ARE NOT YOUR
PROBLEM AS CHRIST SAID LET THE DEAD BURY THE
DEAD - STOP

ADRIAN V

SUBJECT HEADING: I have done as you have asked

Charlie, the one who saved Christendom from Islam, I have done as you have asked. For all intents and purposes, I have run Saint Benedict off the road. I had a special election held. Of course, I won. How could I have lost? If I had, how could the world go on without Saint Peter!

Saint Peter
(MP of the Starry Sphere)

March 26th
Anno Domini 1533

From:
Mr. Arnus (Diviner of the Stars)
PO Box: Eighth Circle of Hell
Apt: Fraud
666

To:
Mr. Ciacco (Gluttonous Banker of Florence)
PO Box: Third Circle of Hell
Apt: Gluttony
666

Comrades,

  lend me your ears. We have lost sight of the mission. The bodies are already rotting, and even Pope Adrian has made the case for the heads not to be reunited with them. If we fail in our mission we will be condemned to Hell again.

Cicacco

From:

Mr. Ciacco (Gluttonous Banker of Florence)

PO Box: Third Circle of Hell

Apt: Gluttony

666

To:

Mr. Arnus (Diviner of the Stars)

PO Box: Eighth Circle of Hell

Apt: Fraud

666

Ciacco,

     I never have known you to be one who is so succinct – good job. Now we must write a chain letter to the Prime Minister, to God, to Dante. We must lobby to the highest authority to get a motion passed to allow safe passage for the barge of bodies below.

Arnus

From the desk of Virgil – Poet and Warden of Old London Bridge

    I am not showing David this communique; it is from the Angels of Heaven. This is the chorus David wishes he could lead. The one that sings unto God perfectly in the heavens. In Purgatory the harmony and melody are not aligned. Harmony can only be achieved when one finishes his sentence, and the melody is the purging that a soul must go through. Things are coming to a head, just read below. I may even be forced to go against my tenants, those I am supposed to serve. Now I really am in limbo. Do I serve Paradise, God's realm which I am never meant to see or serve Purgatory, an imperfect realm but the one that I have the privilege of living in (even though I am supposed to be in Limbo in Hell as I could not accept Christ as my Lord and Savior while living)?

    But enough philosophizing. Let me share a poem.

THE ANGELS

Warm windpipes of mirth sing unto God.
Messengers between the divine and man
that have no autonomy. Happy are they
with their heavenly lot crooning
into God's ear which waxes with pleasure.

To: TheKing@HenryVIII.com

SUBJECT HEADING: Please reconsider

Your Majesty,

Please reconsider your edict stating that the bodies on the barge must pass under Old London Bridge in a fortnight, now ten days. We angels, your choir in Paradise should you return to the fold of morality and lead a better life, beg this of you. We are neither Catholic or Protestant. We have no interests in which faith you profess. We do not favor either the Roman Catholic Church or your newly formed Church of England. Please reconsider for the love of God, so Parliament can get about its business assisting you in running your realms.

In supplication,

The Angels
(MPS of The Primum Mobile)

March 28th
Anno Domini 1533

From:
Office of the Prime Minister
10 Downing Street
London SW1A 2AB, UK

To;
State Parliament
Palace of Westminster
9748 Abington Street
London

Honorable Parliamentarians,

It has come to my attention that the angels have contacted the King. Such an act is not only rebellious, it is treasonous. Therefore, I have expelled them from Parliament. I also am aware that you have been doing some purging of your own. I have heard that Saint Benedict, and Piccarda have also been "forced" to resign. While I am disappointed with you and may have to consider demoting you in my cabinet to lower spheres in Paradise, it is my hope that you can now pass the motion to allow the barge of bodies, the holy martyrs, to pass under Old London Bridge.

God A.K.A Dante
The Prime Minister

To: Justinian@parliament.gov; CMartel@parliament.gov ;
Cacciguida@parliament.gov ; Constantine@parliament.gov;
STThomas@parliament.gov

SUBJECT HEADING: Peter's Pence – or a Fifth Column

Colleagues,

I have received a letter signed by all the souls of hell with a coin at the top of it. I've no doubt that the coin is Peter's Pence to fund the good works that we do on behalf of the country. What I do not know is if there is a fifth column in our midst. The letter petitions us to file a motion to allow the barge to pass under Old London Bridge. The letter also states that all funding from the taxes of Old London Bridge will be cut off if we do not pass such a motion.

With anxiety,

Saint Peter
(MP of the Starry Sphere)

From the desk of Virgil – Poet and Warden of Old London Bridge

Today the messenger, the raven brought his alter-ego a letter from the sphere of the god Mercury. Today I surveyed the bridge, the door by the waterline must be raised, or a flood will ensue. I am going to have to raise the tolls. We pagans consider omens to be messages, so I waited to read the message in the letter from the MP of the Mercury district in the evening. Although brief, the letter wreaks of backstabbing, and were Parliament here in the chapel in which I sit it would have to be reconsecrated. I should also mention that another type of flood has ensured that this morning I had at my door the souls of Parliament that have been "offed." They wanted confession, like Arnus. But unlike my granting the sacrament to Arnus, I have denied them, for who forgives those who plot against God?

JUSTINIAN

King Solomon's heir–
Justinian, the lawgiver.
Seeking to restore Rome
to its former glory, he
will stop at nothing
to achieve this. Even
if he must cut Parliament
in half like the baby.

To: STPeter@parliament.gov ; CMartel@parliament.gov ;
Cacciguida@parliament.gov ; Constantine@parliament.gov;
STThomas@parliament.gov

SUBJECT HEADING: You certainly live up to your name

Peter,

You sure live up to your name! Do you actually doubt that this is a fifth column? If you write that you have any doubts, then you must be a saboteur, a parasite from within. I am tabling a motion to expel you! Now Parliament is down to half of what it was. I feel like King Solomon, only worse, since I have permitted the baby to be cut in half!

Justinian
(MP of The Sphere of Mercury)

ST THOMAS BECKET CHAPEL
OLD LONDON BRIDGE

FROM: KING HENRY VIII

TO: VIRGIL WARDEN OF OLD LONDON BRIDGE

VIRGIL RENAME THE CHAPEL OF ST THOMAS BECKET
TO THAT OF THE APOSTLE IMMEDIATELY! I CANNOT
ALLOW THE CULT OF ST THOMAS BECKETT WHO
UPHELD THE RIGHTS OF THE CHURCH AGAINST THE
KING TO LINGER - STOP -
IT UNDERMINES MY AUTHORITY - STOP - AND WHAT
IS GOING ON WITH THOSE BODIES ON THE BARGE -
STOP

KING HENRY VIII

From the desk of Virgil – Poet and Warden of Old London Bridge

Now I have seen the light! I am going to raise the bridge and let the bodies go through. I
want what Aruns and the souls on Old London Bridge are afraid of. I want to be immortalized in
print, especially my poetry. If I am the one who saves God, who rescues Dante from this
coup, I will get my reward. I will be remembered in not just literature, but in a piece of work that is part of a great literary canon. While I may still be condemned to Limbo, perhaps my verses will be remembered for eternity! The only problem is, the wrench that I need to operate to raise the bridge requires more than one person. Who is going to help me? The souls in Purgatory are not about to, nor are the ones who have taken sanctuary in the chapel. What is a famous poet like me to do? Of course! I must write about it.

REDEMPTION

Is in hand.
A Royal Flush.
I go from the ten in the five-card straight
to one of the faces. A face that I can show
in the halls of Paradise. All thanks to a letter
folded with the waxy seal of the Almighty. Never
mind the King's edict to rename the chapel. If I lose
my head I'll gladly have my body join those on the barge below.

April 1st
Anno Domini 1533

From:
Office of the Prime Minister
10 Downing Street
London SW1A 2AB, UK

To:
State Parliament
Palace of Westminster
9748 Abington Street
London

Honorable Parliamentarians,

I have decided to allow the souls of Hell, the souls that I once banished, to come to Parliament and form a party. I hope that because of my great mercy, they, in their majority, will pass a motion to allow the barge though in order to end this madness. And hopefully these martyrs will also put a stop to your coup which I was aware of all along!

God A.K.A. Dante
The Prime Minister

Heads' Chorus

for Piano

2

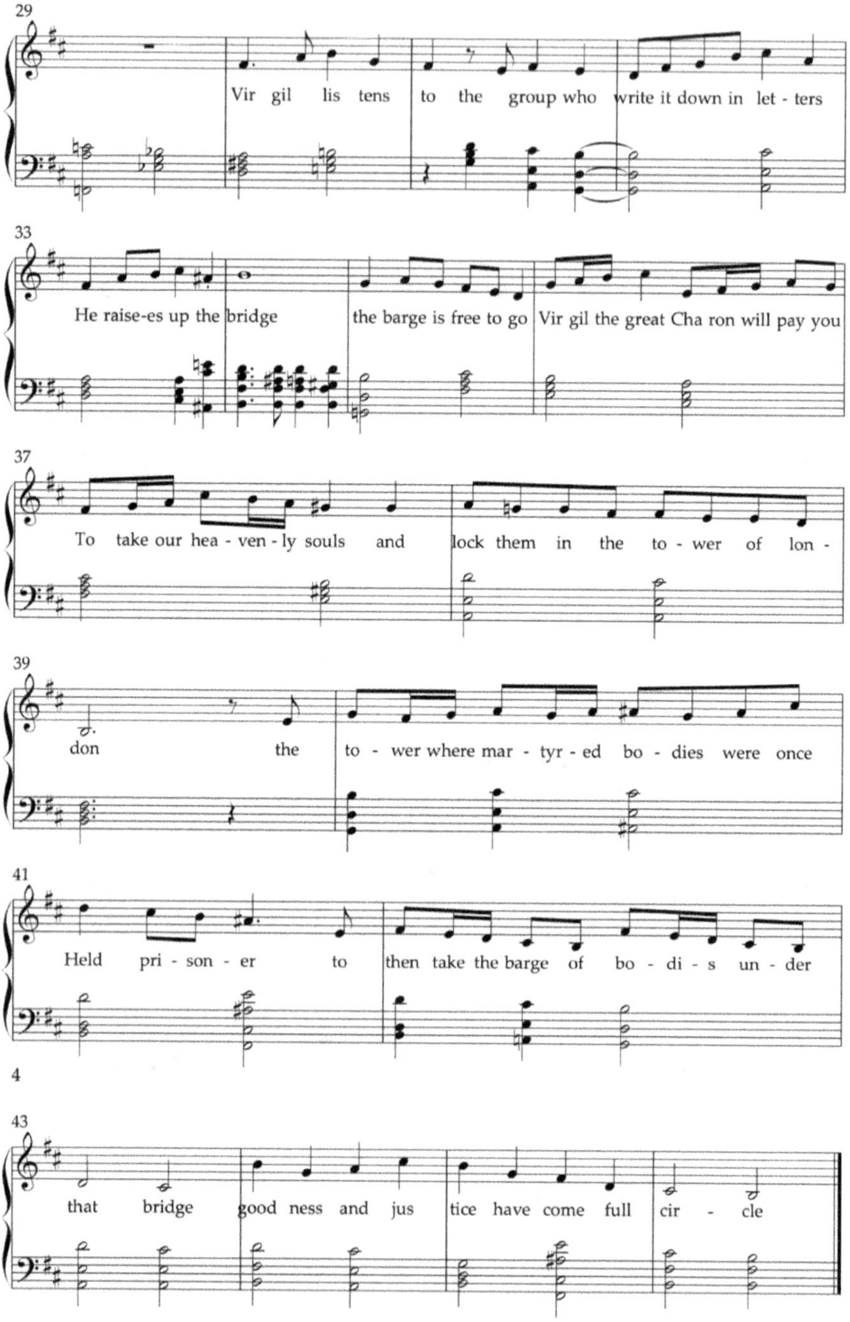
29
Vir gil lis tens to the group who write it down in let - ters
33
He raise-es up the bridge the barge is free to go Vir gil the great Cha ron will pay you
37
To take our hea - ven - ly souls and lock them in the to - wer of lon -
39
don the to - wer where mar - tyr - ed bo - dies were once
41
Held pri - son - er to then take the barge of bo - di - s un - der
4
43
that bridge good ness and jus tice have come full cir - cle

April 12th
Anno Domini 1533

From:
Office of the Prime Minister
10 Downing Street
London SW1A 2AB, UK

To:
Virgil - Poet and Warden of Old London Bridge

My dearest Virgil,

I am sorry that this letter took so long to reach you as it has been a week since Parliament was graced by the martyred bodies and Hellish souls who seem to have reformed somewhat.

I want to say thank you. It is because of this influx of goodness that a new party has been formed by the martyred bodies. It is called Communal Godliness. Tomorrow a vote is to be held which will determine if I keep my throne as God. I know I can win but only with your help. Which leads me to my question: why didn't you send the heads with them. As Plato says a healthy soul can only live in a healthy body, and these bodies that you have graciously provided with me cannot vote without their heads. Please come before Mass on Easter Sunday with the heads. After the celebration I would like to speak with you. I am sending Charon back across the Thames to collect you.

Yours,

God A.K.A Dante

Heads' Chorus

for Piano

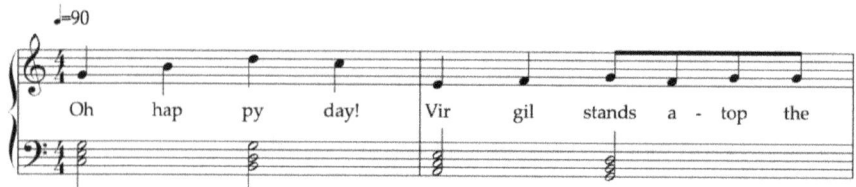

Oh hap py day! Vir gil stands a - top the

prow of Char - ons skiff just like a tri - umph - ant king

jug-gle-ing us as we tra-verse the calm Thames Ri-ver his hands are clam-my with ex

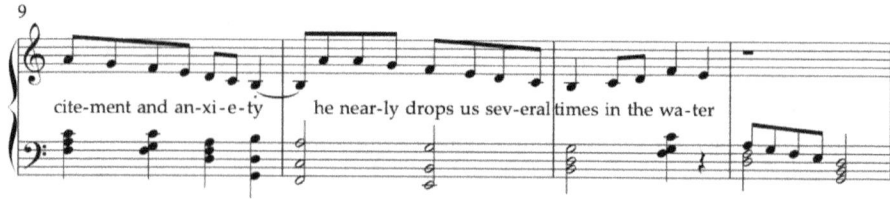

cite-ment and an-xi-e-ty he near-ly drops us sev-eral times in the wa-ter

From the desk of Virgil – Poet and Warden of Old London Bridge

So,

I assume you all want to know how it ended! Well, as always, I have to tell you, in verse.

IMMORTALIZED

And so I make it into print.
Into film, and other media.
Assigned to Limbo as I was not saved–
as Christ came after I was in the grave.
But I am immortalized in Dante's verse,
superior to those of my own pen.
I know not if to cry in sadness or mirth.

www.ingramcontent.com/pod-product-compliance
Lightning Source LLC
Chambersburg PA
CBHW071530100726
47908CB00004B/1349